SHUT ME UP IN PROSE

SHUT ME UP IN PROSE

MAITHY VU

First paperback edition July 2025

Editors: Aubrie Goslin and Cleo Miele

Cover Designer: Zakarias Fariury

Beta Readers: Sydney Fredriksz (*The Daylily Darling*), Dr. Elisabeth Sharp McKetta (title story), Jennifer Fickley-Baker (full), Andrew Peterson (full)

ISBN: 978-0-9963822-2-9 (paperback)
ISBN: 978-0-9963822-8-1 (eBook)
LCCN: 2025705896

To all my sisters—

May they never shut us up.

Contents

The Dead of Light

A mass of blackbirds fell from the sky in the night. Henri didn't know whether they had died midair or were killed by the fall. Either way, a parade of feathered carcasses now lined his neighborhood.

He was almost sure this was her doing. He didn't know how, but he had felt strange ever since he met her.

His brother had warned him about going out alone at night. Ever since they were young, Lyle would tell Henri about the cases he'd heard on the news. Once, a man had been filling up his tank at a gas station when a woman attacked him from behind. Others disappeared from parking lots of convenience stores. The later it was, the more dangerous the women, Lyle believed. But Henri could never focus at home and found it comforting to write in quiet bars over the chaos of cafes during the day.

He mainly went to The Storm Porter, as the newer establishments around town left it quite empty, even on Saturdays. As a result, the owner, Beverly, didn't mind him writing there. She often even let him stay while she tidied up after closing.

Henri was a poet and a playwright who went by the pseudonym of H. Blackbyrd. He knew the name was silly—Lyle had made sure he was aware of that. Both pretentious and pedestrian at the same time, his brother had said, too obviously a pseudonym. Henri didn't entirely disagree. He had picked it in a hurry, then written a fair amount of successful works until it simply became too late to change it.

The night the strangeness began, Henri had slipped a notepad into his satchel, along with a fountain pen and fresh ink cartridges. He had picked twenty-seven pieces of lint off his sweater-vest and cleaned Beckett's litter box. Then he walked out of his oatmeal-colored home and got into his oatmeal-colored car.

It was a particularly nice evening—quite warm other than a slight chill from a breeze. He had driven with the windows down while listening to

Stravinsky. As the air wafted over his face, Henri felt a calm settle in him. He liked being out while others were in bed. It was like the town belonged to him, the road paved specifically for his ventures. It was these sorts of moments that let him forget about the dangers around him. His car provided a sense of security he couldn't feel anywhere else—though when he got closer to the dives, he always made sure to roll the windows up.

Henri pulled into The Storm Porter's tiny lot and turned off the ignition. The streetlamp had been out for weeks, with only the blue neon sign of the bar flickering. There were three other cars, one of them Beverly's. He remembered that he owed her some change from the last time he was there. He started to pull out his wallet to check whether he had enough bills when he was startled by a tap on his driver's side window.

He looked up to see a young redhead, about nineteen or so, offering a smile and a wave. He had no idea where she'd come from or how she got there so quickly, but it wasn't uncommon for women to wander places alone at night. The bars were always filled with them drinking, hitting on barkeeps, or throwing up on the sidewalks. Henri figured she was looking for spare change, so he cracked the window just enough so they could speak.

She said hello and asked for directions to the nearest phone booth, although it was obvious that she didn't really need them. She could have easily gone inside the bar and asked to use their phone. Henri gave her directions anyway. She told him he had wonderful eyes. He thanked her, told her he really must be going now. Were they green? she wondered. Yes, he replied.

He expected her to leave, but she continued standing by his window as though waiting for him to get out. He didn't quite know what to do. It felt odd to open the door and head into the bar with her standing there. And what if she were to follow him inside? It'd be impossible to get any work done then. He could call Beverly and ask her to come outside, but he didn't want to inconvenience her any more than he already did.

She remained there, freckles glowing like stars beneath the moonlight. He didn't know what to do other than turn on the ignition and drive away. The woman watched him the entire time, preternaturally still. He could see her standing there through his rearview mirror even as he sped off.

He'd just have to go to a cafe tomorrow, he thought. He could try to get some sleep, then wake up bright and early. He was not looking forward to the Sunday morning crowd, but he had no choice at that point. The other bars would soon be closing for the night.

The next morning, Henri got into his car and drove to the nearest cafe. When he arrived, he was able to park on the street only a few shops down and discovered plenty of empty seating inside. This made Henri very happy. He purchased a chamomile tea with two lemon scones and chose a table by the window.

Henri told himself he would finish at least three scenes of his play before a friend's birthday party in the afternoon. If he met his goal, he would reward himself with some cake.

He was working on the last scene when a woman approached him. The cafe had grown louder and busier since he'd arrived, so he hadn't noticed her until she was hovering over his table. She acted very kindly, saw he was drinking chamomile, made a comment about how the new bakery down the street served a wider assortment of herbal teas. If he wanted, she could take him there to show him. It would only take a moment.

She was much older than he was, at least twenty years. Not particularly beautiful or ugly—just plain, and not really the sort of woman he would have an interest in. Besides, he wasn't sure if she was flirting or approaching him in a maternal way. Perhaps she had lost a son and felt the need to show affection to a younger man. If this was the case, he didn't want to come across as rude. Lyle always said Henri had an innocent quality that made women want to protect him. He didn't know what it was that made them think he couldn't take care of things himself, but they always offered him assistance of sorts.

He thanked her, told her it was all right, that he'd try the bakery another time. The tea wasn't really a big deal to him; he just wanted to finish his writing.

She nodded, pulled out the chair across from him, and sat down. She asked him what he was working on. He let out a small sigh and told her he was a playwright. She was delighted and began reminiscing over how she had once been deeply involved with the theater. It became clear to Henri that she had no intention of leaving him alone. He apologized, told her he was running low on time and had to be at a birthday party.

She seemed understanding, stood up, and said she'd walk him to his car. He didn't think that was necessary during the day but went along with it, for he just wanted to head home.

When they got to his car, however, he was surprised by the presence of a flat tire. The woman insisted on fixing it for him, but he had left the spare in his garage like a fool. She offered to drive him home to get it. He wasn't fond of that idea, either, but as he glanced at his watch, he found himself giving in.

She didn't talk as much in the car as she had in the cafe, which made Henri a little uncomfortable. Silence was always awkward with strangers, but even more so with a woman who had just talked his ear off. Their conversation mainly consisted of him telling her which turns to make, although at one point she asked him whose birthday he was attending.

When he told her that it was his friend Millie's, she asked whether he was dating her. Henri found her boldness a little irritating. He said no, that she was just a friend, and so the woman asked whether he had a preference for men. He replied politely that he did not and navigated away from the subject by giving her directions.

When they got to the house, she immediately got out of the car and insisted on helping him carry the tire. He assured her that he could roll it out from the garage himself. If she would just stay there, he could run right inside to get it.

She told him that was nonsense. She had already driven him here. It'd be no trouble.

And so, Henri found himself going through the front door and opening the garage as she waited on the other side. The woman tucked one arm into the spare, rested the weight on her shoulder, and tossed it into her trunk.

She was much more talkative on the way back. She asked him if he'd written anything she would have seen. Before he could answer, she asked for his name so she could read his work. He gave her his pseudonym, regretting it immediately as she pulled a crumpled napkin from her pocket and asked him to write it down. He did so reluctantly, his hand struggling to keep the pen steady as he held the napkin up against the rumbling dashboard.

When they returned, the woman replaced the flat with the spare and wished him a wonderful time at the party. Henri thanked her as politely as he could manage and scrambled into his car. He made a conscious decision not to look into his rearview mirror, for he knew he would see her standing there, perfectly still, watching him go. Instead, he stared straight ahead, rubbing his hand against his arm to smooth out the bumps.

Millie was thrilled when Henri showed up at the party. She gave him a welcoming hug and asked if he was hungry. He said yes, pulled her gift from his satchel (two books he had wrapped in newspaper with a bow), and apologized for being late. As she fixed him a plate, he told her all about the woman and the flat tire. She scrunched her eyebrows with concern and warned him to be careful. She advised him how women often gave men flat tires on purpose in order to put them in a vulnerable position. Henri hadn't thought of that.

Millie handed him his plate and told him to call her next time he found himself in such a situation.

Henri had known Millie since grade school. She was one of the few girls he felt comfortable around, because she never asked him on a date or tried setting him up with any of her friends. Whenever she complimented him, it felt sincere, with no intention other than to compliment. She never asked anything of him, and yet was always there to listen whenever he needed a shoulder to lean on.

Millie went around and introduced him to the rest of the party. Some he recognized from school, some were Millie's cousins, and others he had never seen before. Henri dreaded being asked what he did for a living, so he would divert from the subject by remarking on the food or playing with the cat.

When the sky turned a deep blue, Henri grew anxious and bid farewell to Millie. She walked him out to his car and thanked him for the gift.

Millie asked him where he was off to, and he told her he'd most likely head to The Storm Porter to continue writing. He still owed Beverly some money.

She frowned, told him he shouldn't be hanging around those places, made him promise he'd head straight home afterward. He chuckled, told her she sounded just like Lyle, but it was Millie and he couldn't argue. He'd just have to write another time.

Millie opened the driver's door for him and shut it gently as he waved to her through the window. As he drove off, Henri glanced at the rearview mirror and saw that she waited until he got to the corner before going back inside.

The front door was unlocked when he arrived home. For a moment, Henri panicked, thinking someone had broken in. Then he remembered he had let himself in earlier that day to open the garage for the woman. He had forgotten to lock the door when they left.

He swung the door open. All seemed fine, other than the absence of Beckett, who normally greeted him at the door. Henri looked over at her food bowl, which had been eaten from. He called for her, and the feline came wandering in from the bedroom.

Henri let out a sigh of relief. He checked the corners of every room, just in case, for anything unusual. When he found nothing, he had a quick bath and made spaghetti. He had been too shy to get seconds at the party and still found himself hungry.

Henri took his dinner to the living room and sat in front of the television for an hour. When his eyes grew heavy, he shut it off and leaned back in his chair. He thought about what Millie had said, how there were women who caused flat tires on purpose. Could the woman he met have done that? He was safe, so what good would that have brought her? Was it possible that she'd had the intention of hurting him but changed her mind along the way?

He had a sudden thought that she could be lurking outside his home. Perhaps she had parked her car down the street, waited for him to return from the party, then crept behind his rose bushes. She could have been peering through the windows, observing as he drew a bath and prepared his supper in the kitchen. Logically, he knew that was crazy, but the redhead from the night before had caused him jitters that hadn't quite gone away.

He got up. Without looking out the windows, Henri began yanking the strings of the blinds. One by one, they snapped shut. He checked that the front door was locked, then grabbed an iron skillet from the kitchen. In a worst-case scenario, he wouldn't want to *kill* the woman. No—he would knock her out just enough to ensure he could phone the authorities.

He made his way to the bedroom and placed the skillet on the end table. The wind whistled through the cracks of the windowsill. He got into bed and slipped beneath the covers. Beckett hopped onto the bed, curled up at his feet, and kept her head facing the door.

Henri hoped it was cold enough that no one would be able to endure sitting out there. Perhaps the woman had wanted to come but decided against it once she realized how chilly it was.

He picked up the skillet and slid it beneath the pillow beside him.

The next morning, Henri put the skillet back in the kitchen and got dressed. Then he opened his front door to get the paper. A brown paper bag sat in the center of his welcome mat, held shut by a single neat fold.

His heart stopped. He picked it up and peered inside. There was a clear container of homemade biscuits, accompanied by a box of various herbal teas.

He took the bag into the house, locking the door behind him.

How long had it been sitting there? Had she come in the night, or early this morning? Had she put something in them? It had happened to Lyle once, back in school—a girl had offered him a drink, and before he knew it, everything went hazy and dark.

Henri couldn't bear the thought of things being hazy. He never drank for this reason. Even when he wrote late at night, he always ordered ginger ale, despite the looks he received from the barkeeps.

He examined the biscuits, though he wasn't sure what he was looking for. What good would it do her to put something in them? He supposed she could wait awhile, then break into the house once he was incapacitated. She could do what she wanted with him then.

That would be ridiculous, he chided himself. He was sure the biscuits were fine, that she was just being friendly. It was very sweet of her to do such a thing. He could toss them out, to be safe, then lie if he ever ran into her again, tell her they were delicious. But what if that just caused her to give him more? He'd feel awful throwing them out constantly.

He supposed he could take just a small bite. If it did something to him, at least he would be safely inside and wouldn't have had the entire biscuit. He'd get sick, at most. Sick, but not unconscious or dead.

He took a bite, surprised to find it still warm.

During the next few days, Henri finished a rough draft of his play, visited the dentist, and went out of town to visit Lyle.

His brother always pestered him to sell their childhood home and move out of their hometown.

Henri kept reminding him that he wanted to stay for the theaters.

Lyle would shake his head and call it a hunting ground. His wife, Lora, never missed an opportunity to chime in. She'd remind Henri it was no place to raise children, that she was glad she got Lyle out of there. She'd offer to introduce Henri to someone well-off so he wouldn't have to worry about his work. Whenever Henri reminded her that he liked his work, she would scrunch her nose.

Henri spent three days at Lyle's before returning home. It was the longest he wanted to leave Beckett alone, and the longest he could stand being around Lora.

Despite the four-hour drive back to the city, Henri felt refreshed, inspired. It wasn't often that he received these bursts of energy during the day, and it was best to take advantage of such moments. So, instead of heading straight home, Henri decided he'd do some writing.

She was inside the cafe when he arrived, sitting at a table alone and doing nothing other than taking sips from a coffee. His stomach lurched when he saw her.

Her eyes lit up. She immediately stood and went over to him. He got in line, hoping to speed up the conversation by appearing busy.

She asked him how he was, and he answered that he was well and thanked her for the biscuits and tea. He told her that they had been delicious, asked if she'd made them herself even though he knew she had. She said yes, that they were her specialty. Her grandfather had taught her how to make them.

She asked him which was his favorite out of the teas, and he paused because he hadn't opened them. He made up a reason, told her that he still had a selection of his own to get through before opening a new box. Though he added that he was very excited about trying them.

She nodded, seemingly unbothered. And for a moment, he felt relieved.

Then she told him she found him very handsome. She suggested that he come over for dinner.

Henri gulped. It was his turn at the register, so he was able to take a moment to put in his order. He was about to get his usual chamomile but stopped himself and decided on decaf coffee. He could feel her eyes on him, waiting for his answer. He paid the cashier and turned back toward the woman.

She continued by telling him she made a wonderful chicken pot pie. He apologized, told her that he'd prefer not to. He added how he was sure her pot pie was perfect, considering the quality of her biscuits, and hoped the comment would ease her.

She became quiet. He had shortness of breath as the boy behind the counter handed him his coffee. The woman stuffed her hands in her pockets and smirked.

"Blackbyrd thinks he's too good for us, does he?" she said.

Then she stormed out of the shop and disappeared.

So when Henri woke to a mass of dead blackbirds on his street, he was sure it was her. He noticed the first one when he went to check his mailbox. He had shuffled down his driveway in a robe when he felt a soft presence beneath his foot. Henri lifted his slipper and saw the lifeless eyes, twisted head, and shriveled feet. Its beak was agape, as though it had attempted to murmur something before its unceremonious end.

He looked down at Beckett, who had followed him outside. It couldn't have been her. She never went out in the middle of the night, and even if she had, it would have woken him. Beckett let out a meow, and that's when he followed her eyes and gazed out onto the street.

There lay another bundle of black feathers in the middle of the road.

Henri suddenly felt very ill. He scanned his eyes across the neighborhood and saw the dark splotches scattered on lawns, atop hoods of cars, and along the sidewalks—fading into the distance as far as his eyes could stretch.

He scooped up his cat, ran to get his keys from the house, and got into his car. With sweaty palms, he drove to the police station, Beckett scratching at the passenger seat all the while. When he got there, he realized that he was still wearing his robe and feared he would appear even more deranged than he already knew he'd sound. He hoped that the officers wouldn't notice.

Cradling Beckett in his arms, Henri rushed inside the station to the counter, stumbling over his words as he spoke to the two policewomen behind the glass. They asked him to calm down, said that the birds had already been reported, that someone was on their way to clean the mess.

Henri told them that he knew who was responsible for their deaths. The policewomen ignored his statement, informed him that all was being taken care of. He pleaded for them to listen, and so they agreed, though he could tell they were impatient. He told the story as quickly as he could so as not to lose their interest. He began with the cafe, how she had approached him and followed him to his car. He told them about the flat tire and the drive to his home, the biscuits and tea, his pseudonym and its correlation with the birds.

One of the policewomen finally interrupted him by asking for a physical description.

That's when Henri realized he had been so wrapped in his own discomfort, in his own head, he couldn't remember what the woman looked like. Other than the fact that she was older, he couldn't discern her height, whether her hair was curly or straight. All he could remember were the goosebumps across his arms, the iron skillet beneath his pillow, the look in her eyes as he turned her down.

When he couldn't answer, the policewomen chuckled. He had nothing to worry about, they assured him. The incident, though unfortunate, was nobody's doing. The poor creatures had simply been struck by a fireworks display in the night, held by an opera house celebrating its twentieth anniversary.

They commented on his robe, called him a handsome little thing, and suggested that he get some rest.

Little Liability

It wasn't easy getting rid of Marion.

She came to you slowly at first, appearing occasionally as you strolled through the shelter of towering redwoods. It'd be a hello, or a small smile, and though she made you cautious, you had not yet grown to fear her.

As you got to know each other, the smile became a wide toothy grin. When you found a lost fawn on the side of the road, it was Marion who helped you find its mother. When your brother grew ill, Marion sat beside him in the hospital, and whenever your father took your mother's death out on you, it was Marion who stood by your side.

You grew fond of Marion. She introduced you to the feeling of oil paints upon your fingertips, walked you through bursts of red, blue, and black across fresh canvases. She'd play your favorite songs, then dance across each blank slate as you traced your souls—yours and Marion's, Marion's and yours.

You assumed Marion had many friends, that her attention was nothing of concern. It was easier when you didn't think of yourself as special. You told yourself she must do this with everybody.

When you moved to the city, Marion came with. It didn't matter what minds you spent time with; she would always be there right beside you. That's when you thought she found you special after all. You painted every day, Marion's singing as your company.

Your work began to get noticed. You found yourself baffled by crowds staring at your pieces, nodding in approval and murmuring beneath their breaths.

At one of your exhibits, you met Derrick. He caught your eye, for he didn't spend much time at the larger, more elaborate pieces, but rather pondered for a few minutes in front of a modest frame you'd created when you first met Marion.

You approached him, but refrained from introducing yourself, curious as to what he thought.

"There's a youthful yearning in this one," Derrick said. "Blemishes people only dream of having."

You revealed yourself as the artist, and you had him then.

Derrick was patient. Derrick was kind. Even when you mentioned something as trivial as craving strawberry cake, he'd run to the nearest bakery and find you the perfect delight. He'd have silly requests, like insisting you kiss him whenever it rained. He'd leave you alone to paint, sitting peacefully in the corner with a book, oblivious to you glancing up every so often to admire his looks.

Derrick didn't mind that Marion came around. He'd listen to her go on and on about the awful things that happened in her day. You loved Derrick for his temperament, though you wondered whether it was Marion whom he was really interested in.

You'd soon find yourself wrong, as Marion's presence grew to be a problem. Whenever Derrick went off to play cricket, Marion would feed you thoughts, say he was probably meeting another woman. She'd start conflicts with Derrick merely for the sake of starting them. When he whistled a tune in the morning, she'd tell him he was being too loud. When he was too worn for conversation in the evening, she'd say he was too quiet.

Oh, how Marion loved to argue. She'd criticize the way he treated you, accuse him of not being attentive enough, of not knowing who you truly were. Marion was blood boiling, teeth clenching, tears streaming. Eventually, Derrick bit back, claiming she was too demanding, too volatile. So, whenever she was around, you'd tell Derrick not to come over, for fear a fire would start.

Soon, you grew to dread Marion. You wished she'd stop inviting herself to things. Sometimes she'd take herself to your galleries, then embarrass you by spouting nonsense to spectators. You'd stay up all night, tossing, turning, thinking about what Marion had said, wondering whether people thought less of you for her behavior. If the phone rang whenever Marion was around, you'd ignore the call so she wouldn't shout something humiliating. It wasn't long before you avoided going out altogether.

As time went by, Derrick turned cold and quick-tempered. He not only raised his voice at Marion, but he snapped at you, and you began to wonder whether Marion was right. Perhaps he wasn't decent after all, and it took someone like Marion to bring it out of him. Despite that, you couldn't let go of the lover you had met, the one who chuckled and teased and kissed in the middle of thunderstorms.

Derrick fought Marion for twenty-seven months before he grew exhausted. If you didn't do something about it, he threatened, he'd have no choice but to go. You begged her to leave, told her how much turmoil she caused, how much she had ruined your life.

"If he can't handle me," Marion said, "then he doesn't deserve to have you."

Derrick went by his word, and you couldn't blame him. Marion was difficult—there was no denying that. If you couldn't stand having her around, there was no world in which you could expect Derrick to.

You hated Marion. You became determined to make her disappear, trying to think of ways to make her go. You wondered what it was about you that had attracted her in the first place. If you could figure that out, perhaps it would be the key to Marion's end.

You realized you could not do so without help. No, it would take more minds to get rid of her. You attempted to find assistance, pleading with anyone who would listen, but again and again you were told Marion's nature was too ambiguous, convoluted, unfamiliar. Not a single soul could help, and you became convinced you were doomed.

Then came the garage incident. You and Marion had gone to the movies one Saturday morning when you both spotted Derrick. You hadn't seen him in months, had been able to move past your time together, but when you saw the blonde clinging to his neck, laughing and full of life, Marion grew angry. She forced you to head home before the film had even begun, despite having already bought your ticket. As soon as you pulled into the garage, she locked the car doors, left the engine running. You asked her what she was doing. She provided no response, wordlessly rolling down the windows as the garage door screeched behind you, the space growing darker and darker. You fought her for the keys, and she fought back.

"No one will ever love us!" Marion screamed. "We are *unbearable*!"

Marion roared, the engine rumbled, and you sobbed, praying for something different. You had never asked for her, never done anything to deserve her frenzy. You wondered whether she happened upon you by chance, or whether she chose you for your faults. Perhaps you were destined to be together, and this was the only escape. You crawled into the backseat, vision blurring as you lay across it like an open field, stopping between sobs to breathe in the hot poisoned air. And all the while, Marion hummed.

Life began to retire from your lungs, and you were unsure whether Marion was holding you or squeezing her hands around your neck. Stars crept into the edges of your vision until suddenly, the postman, who had heard the soft rumble while dropping off your mail, hoisted up the garage door to find you both—you relieved, Marion livid—with swollen eyes, sticky cheeks, heavy breaths.

The postman dragged you out, your consciousness wafting back to the faint ringing of a phone. You stumbled to your feet and rushed inside, the alarmed postman calling after you. It was your father, as you had thought, muttering those dreaded words.

You pleaded with the postman not to call the hospital—explained how you needed to see your brother. He agreed, reluctantly, if you promised to leave a note in your mailbox upon your return.

You expected her to be there, just like she was for everything else. You thought she'd be on the plane with you, flying over the towering redwoods you once called home. You thought she'd sit with you in the hospital, hold your hand as your tears soaked your brother's soundless chest. But Marion was nowhere to be found. And though you grieved, you were free of her.

Months passed, and still Marion never showed. She didn't call when your father consumed every last bottle in the house, nor did she drop by when you came back to the city. You made new friends, even began seeing Teddy. It was exhilarating without Marion. Without her, there was no one to start petty arguments or interrupt the elation in your heart.

Teddy was simple. Life with him was nothing but adventure and glee. He'd praise you for your independence, say you weren't like the others. He'd make remarks like, "My kind of woman!" and "That's my girl!" He'd make you tea in your own kitchen, sit and listen to memories of your brother. In time, you forgot all about Marion.

You began working in an office. You dressed in suits, stomped down echoing halls in high heels and ruby lips. You were powerful. Your colleagues listened to what you had to say. You visited your father every month and left freshly baked cookies in your mailbox every Saturday for the postman.

One day, Teddy asked you to marry him. He decided you'd both move to the cottage that his folks left behind. So, you cleared out your things, and that's when you found the canvases, leaning against the corner of the closet, dusty around the edges.

You remembered what it was like to press your fingers upon the stretched cotton, palms dripping with color and longing. You took a blank canvas, propped it against the wall, squeezed the half-empty tubes onto the palette.

Then you sat. And sat. And as the canvas remained untouched and the paints began to dry, you realized it was Marion who had chosen the colors. Marion, who held your hands and pushed your stained palms across the white. Marion, who gave you substance, forced you to be strong, let you speak. Marion, who made you intricate, empathetic.

And so you wept, realizing that without Marion, you were nothing at all. Just a speck in an endless landscape, bound to be neglected and forgotten. You despised her madness, but it was her madness that spilled your character.

And it was through this discovery, the paints diluted with tears, and the familiar turmoil in your chest that Marion returned.

Feerday's Fog

Mr. and Mrs. Feerday always had breakfast in their back garden. The only exception was when it rained, in which case, they would have their eggs in the living room. On this day, however, the sun radiated over the vegetables that crawled out of their flowerbeds.

Mrs. Feerday leaned back in her lounger, hoping to get a bit of a tan. She alternated between letting her sunglasses rest on her nose and placing them on her head, because one was much too bright and the other too dark.

On his lounger, Mr. Feerday sat reading a book with his eyebrows scrunched. A notepad rested on his stomach. Once in a while, he would tug at the front of his shirt collar when it bothered his Adam's apple.

"What do you jot down when you do that?" Mrs. Feerday asked him.

"Hm?" he grunted without looking up.

"I just meant—well, who takes notes while reading a novel?"

Her husband shrugged. With a sigh, Mrs. Feerday reached over to the small table between them. She plopped a grape into her mouth and squinted at the sky beyond their stockade fence.

"That's strange," she mumbled through her chews. "Who would be having a bonfire at this time of day?"

"What do you mean?"

"Over there. See the smoke? I do hope it's not a home that's burning."

It was Mr. Feerday's turn to squint, though he couldn't quite see what his wife was looking at.

"I can't quite see what you're looking at," he said. "The sky seems clear to me."

Mrs. Feerday stared at him in disbelief. "How do you not? The sky is nearly gray now. I can hardly see the mountains anymore."

Mr. Feerday grumbled and shut his book. He collected their empty plates and carried them inside.

His wife was left there staring off into the sky, wondering whether her eyes were deceiving her.

Perhaps there was no smoke and there really was nothing to worry about. She had the urge to tell someone, but if they offered the same response her husband did, she'd appear a fool. She decided to ignore it, despite the sliver of uneasiness that prodded her gut.

The next day, Mrs. Feerday tended to her garden and twiddled with her latest project while her husband labored at the scrapyard.

Mrs. Feerday was a lampmaker. She'd made dozens of lamps out of objects Mr. Feerday brought home. Twenty-eight of her creations were scattered around their small abode, the rest given away or sold to local shops. This particular day, she'd made one out of chalkboard and half a globe. She would give it to their son, Luken, the next time they visited him at his university.

When Mr. Feerday came home, she greeted him at the door. He pulled an old fiddle out of his coat and handed it to her.

"Bit broken," he said, kicking off his shoes. "But it might work nicely, eh?"

Mrs. Feerday examined the bent neck, single string, and splintered puncture at the edge of the wood.

"I don't know if I can make something out of this," she murmured. Still, she took it down to the cluttered basement where she kept all her materials. Then she heated up supper while her husband took a quick bath.

After their meal, they took a stroll around the neighborhood. Mr. Feerday always kept his arm around his wife when they walked, which felt especially nice on cold evenings.

"How was your day, dear?" he asked as they rounded a corner.

"Annalise rang," she replied. "She and Gene invited us to their new place this Saturday."

"We haven't spoken to them in a year. What do they want with us?"

"Just dinner," Mrs. Feerday said. "As friends do. We should bring something."

"What do you suggest?"

"A wine, perhaps."

"How about a casserole?"

"We can't exactly bring a casserole to a chef's home."

"A dessert, then?"

"Annalise watches her figure."

"I suppose wine will work."

"I'll bring a lamp as well."

After their stroll, Mr. Feerday put on his favorite record and read in his armchair in the living room. Mrs. Feerday went down to the basement and got to work, where she remained until she no longer heard the record player.

Staring at a pair of ornate doors, Mrs. Feerday hugged a lamp made of cooking utensils against her chest. To her left, Mr. Feerday gripped a bottle of wine in one hand and pressed the doorbell with the other. They had endured a considerable number of headaches deciding on the perfect wine— one they could afford, but fine enough that it wouldn't appear tasteless on their end. Mr. Feerday eventually chose a burgundy he'd tried once at a nephew's wedding.

The doorbell hummed in a way that was less "We're here!" and more "If it's not too much of a bother, we'd very much like to come in, please."

Mr. Feerday drummed his fingers on the bottle. "Quite a house, isn't it?" he murmured.

"Yes," Mrs. Feerday agreed. "Annalise did say Gene's restaurants were doing well."

"The security gate seemed a bit unneces—"

A *click* as the door opened.

"Well, aren't you two a dashing pair!"

Annalise beckoned them inside. A braid swayed across her back, a few strands falling tastefully in front of her face. She wore no bangles on her wrist nor studs in her ears. Her powder-blue silk dress hugged her in all the most pleasurable places, and she was wearing dainty satin slippers as though she'd simply rolled out of bed.

Meanwhile, Mrs. Feerday had spent half the day putting her thinning locks into the perfect bun, painting her face, and finding an outfit that would tastefully hide her gut.

"I've made this for your home," Mrs. Feerday said, holding out her design.

"It's delightful!" Annalise exclaimed. She took it in both hands and held it up to her face, admiring the bulb nestled inside a whisk.

Gene popped around the corner wearing an apron and oven mitts.

"The Feerdays have come to play!" he sang. He gave Mrs. Feerday a kiss on the cheek, peeled off a mitt, and slapped Mr. Feerday on the back with the enthusiasm of a toddler.

"Doll," said Gene to his wife. "Show them the place while I finish up here, would you?"

Annalise led them beneath a long marble staircase. Mrs. Feerday strained her neck trying to see the top of it, wondering how many rooms were on the second floor.

When they reached the dining area, Annalise placed the lamp on a mantel that lined the wall. It appeared small next to the brass candlesticks and antique pendulum clock.

"Lovely fireplace," Mr. Feerday noted, still clutching the wine.

Annalise beamed. "I hope it's not too warm! We like to keep the fire going."

The three sat at the far edge of the long table. Mr. and Mrs. Feerday glanced at the dozen other place settings.

"Oh, those are always there," said Annalise. "Tell me how you've both been! I haven't seen you since the twenty-year reunion! What have you been up to?"

Mrs. Feerday stroked the silver fork in front of her, which sat delicately beside a porcelain plate. "Well, we finished mending the fence in our yard after that storm."

"It *was* quite a storm!" Annalise chimed. "It destroyed the roof of our greenhouse. It took us weeks to find a suitable contractor to rebuild it."

Mr. Feerday placed the bottle on the table. "Would you happen to have a cork s—"

"Ladiessss and gentle . . . man!"

Gene came strutting in with a platter of what looked like seashells collected from the beach. He set it down in front of them with a flourish. "Coquilles Saint-Jacques!"

They feasted on fish soup and escargot and tartiflette, though Mrs. Feerday hoped no one noticed she could barely swallow the snails. She wanted desperately to spit them into her napkin, but it was cloth, so she did her best to chew without letting it touch her tongue.

Annalise and Gene discussed the twenty-eight countries they'd explored and all the exotic dishes they'd tried. Mr. and Mrs. Feerday had always meant to take a trip somewhere but never got around to it after having their son. Though Mrs. Feerday loved Luken, she sometimes envied Annalise for never having children. She and Gene appeared younger than ever with still so much ambition in them. She wondered if they'd ever been tired in their lives.

There was a clatter as Mr. Feerday dropped his napkin ring on his plate.

"Sorry, sorry," he mumbled, placing it back down on the table. Mrs. Feerday noticed a billow of smoke rising from his head.

"Oh my, is something burning in the kitchen?" she asked.

"There shouldn't be," Gene said. "Do you smell something?"

"Oh," Mrs. Feerday replied. "I just thought—the smoke . . ."

The smoke began turning into a dark-gray fog, much like the one she'd seen from their garden. The others stared at her with blank faces.

"You mean from the fireplace?" asked Annalise.

"No," Mrs. Feerday muttered. "I . . . I must have been mistaken."

She looked to her husband, who dabbed his lips with his napkin.

"Excuse me," he said. "I need to use your washroom."

"Just down the hall after the piano room," Annalise directed.

Mr. Feerday shuffled away while Gene rubbed his stomach and leaned back in his chair.

"Have you two gone anywhere exciting?" he asked Mrs. Feerday.

"Oh, n-no. Not yet," she answered.

Gene continued chattering, but she couldn't process his words. The fog grew darker and closer, heightening her awareness of the mantel's ticking clock.

"I better go see if he's all right."

Mrs. Feerday pushed back her chair and hurried into the hall. The fog hovered all the way to the end of it, blinding her as she searched for her husband. She called for him in every room she passed until she reached a staircase descending into darkness. She kept one hand on the railing as she took the steps down, the other outstretched in front of her.

"My love," she whispered. "Can you see me?"

The light switched on. Her husband stood with hands in his pockets, gazing at cabinets upon cabinets of bottles. He turned to her.

"They have a wine cellar," he said.

They spoke not a word in the car. Mr. Feerday's hands never moved from their position on the steering wheel. Mrs. Feerday sat clutching her handbag on her lap, staring out the window.

Even when her husband clicked on the high beams, she still could not see beyond the hood of their car. The fog followed them all the way home and stayed there long afterward.

One morning, Mrs. Feerday woke with the usual heaviness as she opened the curtains of their bedroom window. The fog had hovered around her for so long now, she couldn't even remember what the sky looked like before.

"There isn't anything there," Mr. Feerday insisted as he buttoned his coveralls.

As much as Mrs. Feerday despised the fog, that feeling was nothing compared to the loneliness of being the only one to see it. She hated how deranged she must appear to her husband. The fog was one thing, but the way Mr. Feerday acted as though she imagined it was another. And the more he denied its existence, the darker it became.

"I'll get breakfast started," her husband added.

As he went downstairs, the phone on the nightstand rang. It hardly ever rang this early. Mrs. Feerday hoped Luken hadn't gotten into some sort of emergency.

"Oh, I'm so glad you're there!" exclaimed a chipper voice. "Are you available today?"

Once she got off the phone, Mrs. Feerday ran down to the kitchen with a lightness in her heart and a quickness in her step.

"I may have my first client!" she cried. "Annalise was so impressed by my lamp, she put in a word with a friend who owns a string of hotels. She's helping with the interior design at his new location today and thought I should bring pieces for him to consider!"

Mr. Feerday turned on the stove. "Hm?"

"My lamps . . . in a fancy hotel!" his wife exclaimed. She eagerly filled two glasses of orange juice.

Her husband cracked two eggs into a pan. "That would be something."

Mrs. Feerday had hoped for a bigger reaction. "I don't have time to eat in the garden," she said. "I need to get ready."

She took her glass of orange juice upstairs.

Exiting the grand hotel hours later, Mrs. Feerday wanted nothing more than to disappear. She could feel it—the quivering in her chest, the moisture forming in the corners of her eyes.

"Not here, not here," she muttered to herself. "You've got seven blocks to get through."

Annalise had been so thrilled when she arrived. Yet, as the hotel manager thumbed through Mrs. Feerday's designs, he'd shaken his head.

"These won't do. Thank you for coming, Mrs. Feerday, but unfortunately your lamps aren't compatible with the style of our establishments."

Annalise had apologized to her a thousand times after the manager dismissed himself, blubbering about how they hadn't been seeing eye to eye.

"Your lamps add *character*. I know plenty of others who would love them," she'd promised, but nothing could change the humiliating feeling that clouded Mrs. Feerday's chest. Though it was foggy outside with not a single ray of light, Mrs. Feerday wore her sunglasses all the way home.

In their home, the living room seemed to taunt her. The carpet had more stains than she could count. Blotchy marks sullied the coffee table where a young Luken had scribbled upon it with a pen. The wallpaper no longer showed its checkered pattern—black squares were now fading into the white.

Mrs. Feerday retreated upstairs and slipped into her robe. She went into the washroom and splashed cold water on her face, as though it'd magically drain the swelling.

The light fixture made of coat hangers flickered above the mirror. Once she took in the gray

hairs glimmering throughout her scalp, no amount
of cold water could wash away the uncontrollable
tears that followed.

It wasn't the gray that bothered her—there
were lots of women who looked quite distinguished
with gray hair. Growing old had never worried her.
It was that she had hoped by the time she turned
gray, she would have something to tell.

Yet, as she plucked the brightest strands and
dropped them into the wastebasket, Mrs. Feerday felt
as meager as she had at fourteen.

She looked back in the mirror. It was
fogged—her reflection had become blurred,
formless. She swiped her hand across the glass, but it
made no difference.

Mrs. Feerday shuffled out of the washroom
to the bedroom. The fog left the mirror and followed
close behind as she buried herself beneath the covers.
There it stayed, hovering above the bed where she
slept for the rest of the afternoon.

When evening came, Mrs. Feerday had sunk
so deep into the mattress, she didn't bother greeting
her husband upon his arrival.

"Dear?" he said, coming into the room. "I
brought you a horseshoe."

He touched her shoulder. Mrs. Feerday pulled the covers over her head. She heard a sigh, then a creak as he shut the door.

When he was gone, the fog coiled itself around her body, swallowing her whole. The air left her and she sobbed, praying for it all to stop but knowing it would not.

Mrs. Feerday threw off the covers, but the fog had blinded her. She hobbled across the room, sliding her hand along the wall. She found the doorknob and swung it open as the fog went from gray to black.

"My love," she shouted into the hall. "Can you see me?"

There was no answer. She brought herself to the floor, feeling for the top of the stairwell with her foot. When she found the edge, she slid down each step on her bottom, one by one, until she could not feel any lower. She was so tired now—the fog squeezed tightly, and she wondered whether she should let it take her.

Then, the flicker of a lamp.

She could make out the long boat paddle beside the armchair. It was a standing lamp she'd crafted over a decade ago, when he had first taken her on a rowboat out on the lake. The doorway to the kitchen would be just to the right of it. If she could make it through, perhaps the lamp made of glass jars atop their refrigerator would illuminate the door to the yard.

She stood and made her way toward the light, arms outstretched, wobbling through the living room to the kitchen. The bulbs shone brightly within the glass, and she remembered how the same jars had once been filled with blooming hydrangeas at their wedding. They guided her outside, allowing fresh air into her lungs. She recognized the sound of gardening shears from across the yard.

There he was! She saw him—for a moment— just before the fog swirled around her again. It grew cold, chilling her body as it impaired her sight. And the harder she tried to find him, the darker it got, until he was just a silhouette against the fence they'd built.

"My love," she called. "Can you see me?"

He gave no response, the outline of his body fading faster as the fog froze her insides. She screamed as it bit into her chest. Her fingertips turned numb just before something grabbed them.

"I'm sorry, dear," said Mr. Feerday. "I only just heard you. Did you need something?"

And with that, she burst into tears, her body trembling from the cold as her knees collided with the stone path of their garden.

"I hate it! I hate it! I just want it to stop! Please, stop!"

"Oh," Mr. Feerday said as he rushed to her side. "I'm right here. Hold on to me."

She grasped his shoulder.

"What were you doing out here?" she asked. "I needed you."

"I was gathering tomatoes. Figured I'd make supper today since you didn't seem well. There's this recipe in the novel I've been reading that I thought we could—"

Mrs. Feerday pulled away from her husband and rose to her feet.

"It's fine," she said. "I'm fine now."

She headed back inside, the fog clinging to her body.

Mr. Feerday went after her.

"Are you sure? You seem rather shaken up."

His wife headed toward the darkness of their basement.

"It's nothing. Just let it go."

He followed her down the steps.

"You're obviously upset. Please tell me what's the matter."

Mrs. Feerday reached the bottom.

"I *have* told you," she said. "Many times. You don't believe me."

"I do believe you."

"No, you don't."

"I do. I've seen it."

She turned to face him.

"Y-you've seen it this whole time?"

Mr. Feerday took a moment, giving in to the haze that surrounded them.

"Not always. Sometimes you see it and I don't. Sometimes I see it and you don't. After that dinner at Gene and Annalise's, I had to turn on the high beams because I could barely see the road."

"How could you?" Mrs. Feerday cried. "Do you realize how alone I've been? You tried convincing me it wasn't there!"

Mr. Feerday shook his head. "I wasn't trying to convince you. I was convincing myself. I was afraid."

"Afraid . . . ? Of what it would do?"

"That I couldn't make it go away."

Mrs. Feerday let out a sigh. The cold seeped out of her chest.

"I never needed you to do anything. I just wanted it acknowledged."

Her husband stepped toward her. It had been so long since she'd looked at him for more than a moment. His hair had grown lighter over the years, his eyes troubled, hands aged from working the scrapyard.

"I'm so sorry, my love," he said.

The fog swirled around them. She buried her face in his chest, soaking up hints of scrap metal and familiarity. He embraced her, warming her shoulders as he did on their walks.

Suddenly, Mr. Feerday began to snicker. His laughter echoed throughout the basement, dissolving the darkness that sought to devour them.

Mrs. Feerday wiped her eyes, wondering what had come over him. Her husband attempted words between breaths.

"They had . . . an entire . . . wine cellar!"

She frowned. "It isn't funny. I was so angry at myself. I should've known a chef would—"

"Bottles from floor to ceiling!" he chortled.

And as Mrs. Feerday glimpsed his face, bright red from amusement, she felt the corners of her mouth twitch.

"We spent *four days* deciding on a bottle," she said.

"Four and a half. The last day, you almost made a casserole!"

Then they both laughed hysterically—Mr. Feerday bending over as far as his knees could go, Mrs. Feerday shaking so hard, she was sure she'd lost an inch off her gut. And when their bodies stopped shuddering and air returned to their lungs, Mr. Feerday took his wife's hand and held it flush against his heart.

"May I build a lamp with you?" he asked.

Mrs. Feerday scanned the basement filled with heaps of forgotten objects. She plucked the broken fiddle from a pile and decided it was perfect.

Mr. and Mrs. Feerday always had breakfast in their back garden. Though it contained only a few vegetable plants beside wilted flowers, and the loungers were worn and flimsy, that never seemed to bother them.

Once in a while, a fog would roll in so thick, they'd both become lost within it. When that happened, Mrs. Feerday always shouted for her husband.

"My love," she'd call. "Can you see me?"

"No," he'd reply. "But I'll follow your voice."

~ 59 ~

Gumball on a Sunny Day

Daisie wants to be a veterinarian. Her pet hamster sleeps beside her inside a sock she leaves on her nightstand. She named it Croissant, after her favorite breakfast item.

Daisie wears pink braces across her teeth. She picked the color out herself at the orthodontist's office. It was either that or green. Daisie does not like green.

The other eighth graders tease her about the braces. Daisie is fully aware no one has any desire to kiss her. Even without the bits of sharp metal concealed beneath her lips, she still has bad posture and stringy hair.

Daisie checks out the latest fantasy novel

from the school library. She bites her nails as she reads it during physical education. Coach tells her to put it away and makes her run laps.

Daisie is sweaty after running laps. She changes out of her gym clothes and puts on jeans and a purple T-shirt two sizes too big. The shirt was handed down to her by a cousin. Daisie stuffs her jacket into her locker on the way to art class.

The art assignment of the day asks students to paint their deepest fears. Some splash guts across car crashes and bus accidents. Others depict spiders with sweeping black strokes. The popular girl draws a snake. Daisie paints a portrait of herself as an adult with braces.

After finishing their paintings, the kids crowd the classroom sink, scrubbing their hands. Daisie tries to scrub the hair off her arms until they turn bright red. The class clown laughs and calls her a lobster.

At lunchtime, Daisie spots the new kid who moved here from a country she cannot pronounce. The girl is alone under a tree on the edge of the courtyard. Daisie sits down cross-legged beside her. They don't speak the same language, but they share fruit snacks.

In literature class, the teacher says he'll be giving out participation points. He encourages everyone to raise their hands to contribute to the discussion. After listening to others' thoughts, Daisie musters up the courage to raise her hand. The teacher calls on Bethany. Bethany makes the same comment that Daisie had in mind. Daisie lowers her hand. She does not receive participation points.

After her last course of the day, Daisie stops by her locker to grab her jacket. It's yellow with a giant smiley face embroidered on the back. She puts it on and heads outside by the bike racks.

Daisie munches on pretzel sticks as she waits for her father. She watches as her peers get picked up, one by one. None of them act excited. They groan and reluctantly say goodbye to their friends as they shuffle toward their parents' cars. Daisie can't relate. She loves spending time with her father. Sometimes, if he's had a bad day, they head to the diner for milkshakes before going home. It spoils their appetite for dinner, but Daisie's mother doesn't get angry. She just shakes her head and wraps their plates in tin foil.

When her father doesn't show, Daisie decides to walk home. She crunches on the rest of her pretzel sticks as she shuffles off campus down the road. It's a sunny day with a nice breeze. Daisie has never walked home before, but it doesn't feel very long in a car. She's sure it will take her less than thirty minutes.

On the way, Daisie passes by the strip mall. There's a gumball machine outside the convenience store. She remembers she has a quarter in the side pocket of her backpack. She pulls it out and wanders toward the machine.

Daisie slips the quarter into the slot and turns the handle clockwise. A blue gumball drops through the chute. She pops it in her mouth and breaks the hard surface with her back teeth. Someone taps on her shoulder.

The boy is older than her and has a chipped tooth. He tells her he likes her jacket. Her cheeks turn red as she thanks him. They're redder than her arms in art class.

The boy points at the mechanical pony and asks Daisie if she wants a ride. He has a quarter in his shoe. She sits on the pony's back while he stands on its front legs, facing her. The boy slips in the coin and clutches the pony's ears. They laugh as it rocks to the tune of *The Lone Ranger*.

When the pony stops, they take in its stillness. The boy remarks that Daisie's breath smells like raspberry. She says it's the gum. He tells her she's not supposed to chew gum with braces. She spits it into her palm.

The boy gives Daisie her first kiss. It feels like clouds and stars and moonbeams. Time slows while her heart races. She makes a note in her mind to write all about the moment in her journal as soon as she gets home. The kiss ends. She still has the gum in her hand.

The boy helps Daisie off the pony and asks her if she needs a ride to her house. His father is inside the store and will be out soon. They can drive her home. She agrees.

The boy's father exits the store with a plastic bag filled with things he purchased. Daisie tosses the gum into a trash bin. She follows the boy and his father to their van. There are only two seats, so they tell her she'll have to sit in the back.

Daisie does not realize how dark it will be until they slide the door closed. She tries to ask them if they could turn a light on, but they don't answer.

Daisie fumbles for her turtle keychain that illuminates when she presses down on the shell. The keychain light is dim, but she can make out some tools and paint cans. There's a crumpled-up fast food bag and an empty soda cup from the burger place by her house. She can smell the corn oil left behind by consumed french fries. The van starts to feel hot and stuffy.

Daisie knocks on the plastic barrier behind the boy and his father. She can't see them, but she can hear muffled conversation. In a polite voice, she asks if they can turn on the air-conditioning. They turn on the radio instead.

Daisie brings her knees to her chest and traces her fingers over the rips in her jeans. The holes and frayed edges of the denim hold her history, like a creased map yellowing with time. She starts to feel a rapid thumping in her chest. She closes her eyes and thinks about Croissant.

Daisie is found dead on a Wednesday morning. The announcement is made on the intercom at school. Kids who never spoke to her shed their tears while teachers do their best to comfort them.

The police keep Daisie's yellow jacket. They interview everyone at school, including the janitor and bus drivers. No one remembers seeing Daisie after classes ended that day.

Daisie's parents refuse to speak to anyone. They shut themselves in their house while news reporters litter their lawn like birds pecking for worms.

Daisie is the only subject people talk about for weeks. They mutter phrases like "darling thing," "so much potential," and "her poor mother." They leave flowers and freezer meals. They hold their children tight and don't let them wander alone.

Daisie's body is buried in the town cemetery underneath a yew tree. Dandelions sprout in clusters around her grave. They are the only dandelions in the entire thirteen-acre yard. The groundskeeper can't come up with an explanation for it.

Sunny days turn to rainstorms, and conversations turn to the weather. People worry about flooding. They lay sandbags along their houses. News reporters bundled up in trench coats grip wet microphones. They shiver as they spout phrases like "nasty out here," "treacherous roads," and "coming in waves."

Daisie's name no longer rings throughout the town. The rain ceases. Everyone is relieved they've avoided a hurricane. Kids at school chipper with excitement about the upcoming spring formal. They whisper names of who they'd want to dance with and giggle when their crushes pass by them in the hall.

The coach's son has his eye on a girl named

Iris. The other guys feed him ideas on how to ask her to the dance. They help him spray-paint a giant sign.

Iris wears green braces across her teeth. She picked the color out herself at the orthodontist's office. It was either that or pink. Iris does not like pink.

Iris wants to be a singer. She taught herself how to play keyboard and writes songs about the girl who sits three seats away from her in advanced algebra. The girl wears blue nail polish and always has perfect curls. Iris thinks about asking her to the spring formal.

Iris decides she wants a sequined dress she can dance in. She sneaks out of school during lunchtime to go shopping. When she gets to the discount clothing store, she sees the clerks locking up the doors for their lunch break. She asks them what time they'll be back, but she can't hear their answer over the rousing tune of *The Lone Ranger*.

The Ferig Express

The first thing Ross did after her divorce was finalized was take the Ferig Express from Adelin to Cape Teccan. She had been on many trains before that didn't get her where she wanted to go, but she was certain this time would be different. This time, she had no expectations. She hadn't planned her trip, packed any bags, or told anyone she was going away. No, she had walked right out of the courthouse with five dollars in her purse and headed straight into the station.

Ross was the type of woman who put care into certain aspects of her look and not so much in others. She was sixty-two and wore too-white powder over the lines and rosacea on her cheeks. Her nails were painted, but her hair wasn't combed. Her coat had decorative gold buttons, but her shoes were worn as she shuffled across the platform on this very day.

After spending a dollar on her ticket, Ross boarded her new refuge and chose a seat by the window. The cabin was empty other than the steward, who stood by the door and tipped his hat as she entered. There were booths on each side of the aisle, with tables sandwiched between seats that faced each other. She supposed this arrangement was for dining purposes. She hoped no one would sit across from her.

Ross picked a booth in the back, placed her handbag on the seat facing the doors, and slid beside it. She watched as the steward greeted arriving passengers. Some traveled alone, some were in pairs, others with their families. If any of them tried to speak to her, she thought of giving a fake name. That was the thing about trains—once aboard, you could be anyone you wanted to be.

By the time the doors closed, there were only three people sharing her cabin, all on the other side of the aisle. One was a man about half her age— sitting alone in his booth—nearly asleep with his head resting on the window beside him. Two booths away from the man, a mother clutched a pet carrier on her lap. Her daughter—about ten years old—sat across from her, reading a book.

As the voice on the intercom announced the train's departure and the wheels began to chug along the tracks, Ross could see the black nose of a small Yorkshire terrier sticking out of the carrier. She watched as the mother shushed its whines. The man woke from his slumber, peeling his face away from the window and gazing out at the blur of the city whizzing by.

Ross shut the curtains of her own window. She pictured Arthur walking out of that courthouse with a smug look on his face, heading to the nearest deli to grab a ham on rye. He'd ask for extra pickles and top it all off with a cucumber soda to celebrate. He wouldn't miss her yet. No, he'd love this first day alone.

Ross peeled a piece of loose skin from the side of her thumbnail. The spot grew red.

He'll come around, she told herself.

The steward began making his way through each cabin to check passenger tickets. When he got to her, he gave her a smile.

"Ticket, ma'am?"

She pulled it from her bag and handed it to him.

"How long until Cape Teccan?" she asked.

"It is the last stop," he replied. "There are three before that one."

"How long do those take?"

"As long as it takes."

He gave the ticket back to her.

Ross sighed. She had hoped to get to her destination immediately. She wasn't looking forward to having stops along the way. But then, she realized, perhaps that might not be a bad thing after all. Perhaps Arthur would be there at the next stop— had taken a taxi to catch up to her and was standing on the platform with roses and sorry eyes. It'd be unlike him, but she wouldn't be surprised by anything these days.

Would she want that? Part of her did, but the other part wished she'd never see him again. No, that was harsh—of course she'd want to see him.

The steward gave her another smile before he wandered off.

Ross had been an aspiring actress when she first met Arthur. He'd convinced her that she was being too ambitious.

Do you have any idea what you're up against? he'd said. *There are thousands out there trying to do what you're doing. Gorgeous broads who might as well all be models.*

The remark always stung a bit, as though he were implying she wasn't beautiful enough, but she knew he didn't mean it that way. He was a practical man. She would have done foolish things if it weren't for his good sense. She was glad he had kept her grounded. It had probably saved her from a lot of heartbreak and shattered dreams.

Suddenly, there was a faint smell. It was a strange aroma unlike anything Ross had ever experienced before. The closest thing she could think of to describe it was fresh onion. It most definitely didn't smell like sweet grilled onion you'd find on a steak. No, it was sharp and stinging—the kind they'd toss into a sad salad of lettuce and tomato.

She looked around. No one was eating anything, and no one else seemed to notice. Perhaps someone was cutting onions in the next cabin over, though that'd be a peculiar thing to do on a train.

Ross decided to ignore it and fell asleep.

When she woke, there was a steaming cup of Earl Grey and a cucumber sandwich on the table in front of her. The bergamot wafted into her nose and made her forget all about the smell she'd noticed earlier. She rubbed her eyes and saw the steward walking away, pushing the cart down the aisle toward the next cabin. She picked up the tea, blowing across the surface to cool it, and stared at the cucumber sandwich for a moment. She wasn't hungry. It reminded her of Arthur.

"Are you going to eat that?"

Ross looked over at the man in the other booth, who had already devoured most of his own. He pointed at her plate, still chewing with cheeks full.

"Oh," said Ross. "No. You can have it."

She held up the plate.

The man swallowed his bite, stood from his seat, and wandered across the aisle to her. Instead of taking the plate, he sat down on the other side of her table. She put the plate down and slid it toward him.

He held out a hand. "Peter."

"R—Ruby."

They shook hands before he picked up the sandwich. "Thanks, Ruby."

"You're welcome," she said, her insides tingling with adrenaline. She wondered how long she'd have to keep up her lie.

"Not a fan of cucumber?" Peter asked.

"Not really," she replied.

"Me neither."

"What? Then why are you eating it?"

"It was my sister's favorite."

Peter took a bite and pushed the curtain away from the window.

"Oh, please don't do that," said Ross. "I'm trying not to look back."

"I'm sorry. I can't help it," said Peter, shutting the curtain. "I keep thinking she'll show up and tell me it was all a joke. She was my best friend."

A tear fell onto the plate. Peter wiped his eyes and went back to the sandwich.

"And who's the reason for your being here?" he asked.

Ross cleared her throat. "M-my husband. Well, I suppose he's not my husband anymore. He's not dead. He's just—"

"Gone."

"Right. But perhaps not forever. I mean, one never knows—"

Ross was startled when Peter took her hand, but after a moment, she rested in the quietness. He moved his hand back to the sandwich.

"Was he your best friend?" Peter asked with his mouth full.

"Of course," Ross replied. "We were married for thirty years."

"That doesn't mean anything."

That doesn't mean anything, Arthur once said when she'd won a poetry contest from the local newspaper. *They pick whoever will make the best story. Middle-aged housewife with no past achievements . . . people like underdogs.*

"If you've finished your sandwich," Ross said to Peter, "could you leave me alone?"

The bulge in Peter's left cheek twirled as he chewed. "I didn't mean to insult," he said. "I was trying to understand your situation."

Ross crossed her arms. "My situation isn't yours to understand. I never even invited you to sit here."

"Whoa, whoa. No need to get testy," Peter said, throwing up his hands. "I was just making conversation."

"I don't need conversation."

"Cranky old bat."

When Peter returned to his seat, the faint smell of onion returned to Ross's nose.

"Probably coming from that ungrateful sandwich-hogging wanker," she grumbled.

Who had a best friend at this age, anyway? The concept was elementary. Everyone had their own unique purpose. To say one was more special than the others would be childish.

She felt the train slowing down.

Gerald's new wife is hosting a birthday party for him this Saturday. I know you're tired from our outing last weekend, but it'd be impudent if we didn't show. He is my best friend, after all.

Arthur hadn't even looked at her as he took off his shoes and slid them under the bed. Ross remembered sliding across the mattress to move closer to him.

I suppose it gives me an opportunity to wear that blue dress I like, she'd replied.

No, that won't do, Arthur insisted, grabbing another from the closet.

That? she said. *I wear that dress to funerals. It doesn't seem appropriate for a celebration.*

You've gotten a little wider in the hips, though, haven't ya? Best if we go for black.

The stench was so strong now, it nearly made her gag.

"Excuse me," Ross said to the mother, who was feeding the terrier bits of bread through the carrier. "Do you smell that?"

The little girl put down her book. "Are you talking about the tea?"

"No," said Ross. "It's more like onion."

The mother shrugged. "I'm afraid we don't know what you mean."

"Maybe I do smell it now that she's said so," said the little girl.

"No, sweetheart," said the mother. "It's just your imagination."

Ross huffed. "How do you know? She may very well smell it too!"

"Please don't speak for my daughter. Why don't you just keep to yourself?"

The train came to a halt.

"STATION STOP AT GRENA!" the steward announced over the intercom.

The doors slid open. The dog barked. The girl covered her ears and wailed.

"Oh, stop that! You're not a baby anymore!" her mother scolded.

"I miss Father! Why can't he come back? I want Father!"

The mother turned to Ross. "Look what you've done!"

"LAST CALL FOR GRENA!"

The mother stood, one hand clutching the carrier, the other gripping her daughter's arm.

"Grab your things," she told the girl. "We're getting off here."

"But Mother, I want to keep going!"

"Hush!"

Mother and daughter shuffled down the aisle and disappeared out the doors. Ross was tempted to pull back her curtain to watch them leave but decided against it.

"Wow, Ruby," said Peter. "Not only are you incapable of conversation—you've now made a child cry over her dead father. Well done."

Ross sucked on her teeth. "Why don't you move to another cabin if I'm so horrible? There are plenty of empty seats."

"My god, you're sensitive. Is no one allowed to use sarcasm anymore? Who made you like this?" Peter poured himself a cup of tea. He dropped in a cube of sugar and stirred violently, the spoon clanging against the glass as tea splashed all over his sleeve.

"If you ask me," he continued, "I'd say you need a drink and a very long nap." He stopped stirring, sucked the spoon, and let it clatter onto the table.

"What I *need* is for you to stop belittling me."

"Ah, so you're turning this around on me, are you?" said Peter. "Somebody's brave enough to call you out for being rude, so now they're the ass?"

Ross thought for a moment. Perhaps Peter was right. What was she thinking, bothering a poor mother and daughter about a silly smell? It wasn't their business to worry about. They had been doing perfectly fine, and she'd disturbed their trip and forced them to hop off the tr—

"No!" cried Ross. "You will not do this to me! I know what this is . . . I've heard about it. It's called . . . there's a word for it. I remember. It's from a play . . . it's . . ."

Light the fireplace, will you, Ross?

Arthur tightened the sash of his robe around his waist, muttering. *Freezing in here.* He plopped down onto his Chesterfield chair and crossed his slippered feet upon the ottoman.

Ross coughed as she went over to the fireplace. She was so prone to colds that time of year. Arthur watched as she turned on the gas and tossed in a match. They waited. The flame remained its size.

You stacked the wood all wrong. It won't spread.

Silence devoured her as she poked at the wood with a fire iron. After a moment, Arthur growled. *Forget it. Give it to me. I'll do it.*

He grabbed the iron out of her hands and stabbed the wood. It hissed and spit out a spark. Ross cried out as the ember hit her wrist.

Oh, don't exaggerate, Arthur snarled. *You were nowhere near it. It couldn't have flown across the room, now, could it?*

The flames grew. He put down the iron and stood staring at the blaze with both hands on his hips.

There ya have it, he'd said proudly. *Now come sit with me, my dear.*

Arthur had a way of altering any room he was in. Whatever air he wanted others to breathe, he'd have the power to do so. His moods were hers. If he told her the sky was green, she'd believe him.

So when Ross's wrist bloomed with a small blister late that night, she told herself she'd burnt it on the stove making winter stew.

"Do you think they'll make me a strawberry tart if I ask nicely?" said Peter.

The smell had returned, sharper . . . overpowering. The train rumbled and squealed. Teacups shook upon their saucers. The steward appeared from the front cabin with his cart to collect them as they trembled.

Ross yanked back the curtain of her window. Charcoal clouds crept toward each other. A bolt of lightning shuddered against a dark sky.

She ran from her booth, burst into the cabin behind them, and slid the door shut. There was no noise other than the rumbling of the train wobbling on its track.

The silence began to devour her. She let out a raging scream.

When the sound that came from the depths of her subsided, she was unsure whether it'd actually made her feel any better. If anything, it had just given her the urge to scream again. So she did.

"Well, if *that* doesn't do the trick," said a voice.

Ross hadn't noticed the woman sitting in the far booth.

"I—I'm so dreadfully sorry," Ross stammered. "I thought this cabin was empty."

The woman had lavender hair that fell beyond her waist. Ross had never seen hair so beautiful. It reminded her of the water nymphs in books from her childhood.

"Not to worry," the woman said. "We all need to let it out every now and then."

"Still," replied Ross. "I—I'm so embarrassed."

"If we didn't have problems, we wouldn't be here."

Ross let out a breath. "Why are you here?" she asked. "If you don't mind my—"

"My daughter," said the woman. "The court granted her father custody."

"I'm sorry."

"It's probably better that she's with him. He'll find a new wife, and she'll have a new mother. Women are so willing to care for someone else's child."

Ross turned to one of the windows. They were far outside the city—only yellow grasslands greeted them now. Raindrops glowed beneath the sun as they fell, hitting the panes so gently that they made no sound. The train stopped swaying.

"What will you do, then?" she asked the woman.

"I don't know. Become better, I suppose. Perhaps he'll let me see her if I do things the way he wants me to."

Ross nodded, stretching her lips with sympathy. She ambled down the aisle to the woman's booth.

"Those are beautiful playing cards," she said.

The woman picked up the deck. "They're not playing cards. They show your future. Care to try?"

"My future?" Ross laughed, thinking it a joke.

When the woman gestured to the empty seat in front of her, Ross realized she was not joking at all.

"You mean the cards are magic?" Ross asked. She slid into the empty seat and twisted her hands.

"STATION STOP AT BIGGARA INN!"

"Ask a question," the woman said, "in your head." Her hair glimmered against the sun rays that pierced the glass beside them.

The question came to Ross quickly.

Will he come around?

She pretended to ponder for a moment before giving a nod.

The woman shuffled the cards and asked her to cut the deck. Ross wouldn't have known what that meant if Arthur hadn't constantly practiced his card tricks on her back in the day. He was always eager to show off his illusions. Their bedroom closet was filled with hats, plastic wands, and scarves all tied together in endless ropes. It drove her mad at times, especially when she'd be searching for her silk flower brooches and have to weed through feather bouquets.

"LAST CALL FOR BIGGARA INN!"

Ross cut the deck.

The woman shuffled again until a card spit itself out onto the table. She turned it over.

"Ah, the parasite. An affair full of poison."

She pulled another card.

"The dying tree. It is the end."

She pulled a third.

"The wolf. You may walk alone, or, if you choose, in a . . ."

The woman's voice faded into noise as Ross thought of Arthur's vows. She remembered how he'd promised to love all her faults and rub her feet every time she'd had a long day. *We'll keep the stockings on if they smell*, he'd teased as the guests chuckled in their seats.

She should have reminded him of those days. She should have pulled out the photo albums and played the songs they used to dance to. Why hadn't she done any of that?

She was too cowardly to stand up to the person he'd become. If she could go back, she'd try harder. She'd make him remember. She'd recreate their wedding cake and squeeze into her old dresses. She'd get a dog and train it to follow him around. She'd take a thousand fertility pills until they gave him a child.

"Please try another card," begged Ross. "I don't think they were shuffled enough."

"The cards don't lie."

"Perhaps just one more time? I promise I won't ask again. Just one more card?"

"You cannot change your fate."

"Here," Ross pleaded, digging in her handbag. "I can give you two dollars for another reading."

"For God's sake, Ruby, put your money away," said Peter, who had wandered in from the other cabin. He leaned against the doorway, arms crossed. "You're embarrassing yourself."

"What are you doing here?" Ross snapped. "Did I not tell you to leave me alone?"

"I came to apologize," Peter said. He walked down the aisle toward them and put his hands in his pockets. "I shouldn't have called you an old bat."

"A *cranky* old bat."

"Well, you were cranky. Just not old. Or a bat."

Ross rolled her eyes.

"Look," said Peter. "I'd hate to think that this train can turn me into someone I don't like. Give us one more chance?"

The lavender-haired woman gathered her cards into a pile and slipped them into a drawstring bag. "I'll leave you two alone," she said, standing from the booth and moving to the far one by the doors.

Ross leaned back as Peter slid across from her. They sat in the silence, and for the first time, Ross didn't feel like it would swallow her.

"You remind me of Penelope," said Peter. "It's probably why I was so harsh."

Ross watched his mind leave her for a moment.

"When did you lose her?" she asked him.

He came to. "Three years ago."

"You—you've been on this train for three years? But that's impossible. Isn't this the express?"

"Time means nothing on this thing, Ruby. They say it does, but it's all lies."

Ross felt a lump in her chest. "I don't want to be here that long," she said. "How do I make sure I don't get stuck? Will the steward help me? Perhaps if I pay him? I can give him three dollars."

"It doesn't work that way," said Peter.

Warmth dissipated from the air as the windows turned cloudy. Ross began to sweat against the cold. What if she never reached her destination? What if she remained on the train and it went around and around like one of those toys beneath a Christmas tree?

"Stop worrying," Peter told her. "You should be proud of yourself."

"I don't feel proud."

"You will."

The setting outside disappeared before they could acknowledge it. Peter touched the frozen glass. His hand left a mark.

"I should have been there," he muttered. "I should have—I should have been there to help her."

"STATION STOP AT SERIES POND!"

The doors opened.

"I'm afraid I must get off at this stop," he said.

"What? No!" Ross cried. "You mustn't. What if you can't get back on?"

"I don't care anymore."

"You need to stay if you want to reach Cape Teccan. Don't you want to see the ocean?"

"There is no ocean."

"You're being silly. Of course there is!"

"I'm sorry."

"LAST CALL FOR SERIES POND!"

"Peter, please."

"Good luck, Ruby."

Peter walked to the open doors, rubbed his hands in the cold, and made wisps of white with his breath. Ross watched as he stepped off the train and into the gloom. The doors closed.

Ross rushed to the window, her hands quivering as she slid open the frosted glass.

"Peter!" she called.

He turned, his face blurry within the haze.

"It's Ross!" she shouted. "My name is Ross!"

The train whistled and stretched the distance between them. Peter put up a hand.

"Goodbye, Ross!"

As the floor beneath her trembled and she could no longer make out the dark outline of her friend, Ross felt herself being swallowed again.

"Don't you worry," said the lavender-haired woman. "He'll find his way."

Ross shook her head. "How do you know?"

"There are things beyond what we can see."

The woman held up a card. Displayed on it was an image of a jellyfish.

Ross didn't feel like bothering with that nonsense anymore. She scoffed and exited the cabin to retreat back to hers, where she found a strawberry tart at her table.

She could do nothing but stare at the pastry. Ross was afraid of Series Pond, and she certainly didn't want to go through it without Peter. Why did he have to leave her? He was just like everyone else, running off when things got difficult. Still, she missed him. He might have been a new acquaintance, but he had understood her more than anyone she'd been close to. What would happen to him? Would he stay there forever?

Stop that, Ross told herself. Why must she be so dependable on others? Surely, she'd done things alone before. She tried to think of something she'd been capable of accomplishing on her own, but her mind kept drawing a blank.

It was then that she realized she could not remember who she had been before she was Arthur's wife. Who was that woman? Did she sing? Did she collect seashells? Did she pick up pennies she found on the ground? What did she fear before she feared his temper? What made her laugh before receiving his taunts? What made her cry?

Ross wept over the tart. She buried her head in her hands, forcing her mind to think harder.

What films were her favorite? Did she go to the cinema with her friends? Who were her friends? What books did she read? The water nymphs! Yes, she remembered those. Did she spend her summers at the lake? Did she swim in it? Did she like the way her body looked in a swimsuit? What foods did she enjoy? Did she like the taste of strawberry?

She picked up the tart from the table and bit into it. It tasted like onion. She sighed as she put it down and let her head rest against the icy window. Still, she could not see outside.

The train continued onto the tracks built over frozen water. Ross heard the ice crack beneath them. Would it give way? Would they all fall under? And what of Peter? Had he already lost himself to the abyss?

She laid herself across the seat and curled her knees to her chest. Her head rested on her handbag. Ross understood then that she did not mourn the end of her marriage, but the parts of her that had been lost because of it.

Her eyelids swelled from the salt of her tears. She shut them until she fell numb and heavy into sleep.

When she woke, Ross was greeted by the faint smell of sweet pea. Her eyes opened slowly, and she wondered for a second whether it came from a dream. Realizing it did not, she stumbled out of her booth and followed the scent. It grew stronger as she made her way down the aisle. She slid open the doors to the next cabin. It was empty. She crossed that one and slid open another. Empty. The smell encased her now. She stumbled toward the next set of doors, hands fumbling over the headrests of seats on each side of her.

She slid open the doors of the last cabin. There, she discovered a greenhouse. Ross stared in awe as the glass walls revealed the shifting landscape outside. Bare trees moved at mesmerizing speed into ones full of foliage. The glossy ice pond melted into a sparkling blue, and the sun formed dancing reflections upon the water.

In the center of the room, the steward stood surrounded by flowers, humming as he trimmed their stems.

"You'll have to excuse me," said Ross. "I couldn't help it. The smell was . . . enchanting."

"Ah, you've discovered our gifts," the steward replied. He held out a bouquet. "For you, ma'am. To take with you to Cape Teccan."

Ross took the arrangement of sweet peas and buried her nose in the center. She watched as the steward filled a cart with dozens of bouquets.

"May I ask you something?"

"Of course, ma'am."

"Will I come around?"

"Of course, ma'am." He placed the last bouquet on the cart. "Would you like to deliver them with me?"

Ross nodded. She followed the steward closely as he pushed the cart into the next cabin. Aisle by aisle, they handed bouquets to passengers in cabins she'd sworn were empty before. There were also empty seats that were once filled. Eventually, they reached the woman shuffling cards in her hand. Ross handed her an array of lavender blossoms that mirrored her hair.

"I'm sorry for leaving suddenly before," Ross said. "I wasn't ready for the truth."

The woman plucked a flower and nestled it behind her ear. "I was hardly ready myself. But we've made it, haven't we?"

When every passenger had their bouquets, the steward pulled the cart all the way back to the greenhouse. Ross gazed down at the glass floor. Specks of sand flew on either side of the track as the wheels chugged along. She looked out the walls and saw palm trees, long-winged birds, foamy waves crawling in and out of shore.

As the train slowed to a halt, the steward removed a powder-blue phone from its receiver mounted to the farthest wall.

"STATION STOP AT CAPE TECCAN!" he announced. He hung up and turned to Ross.

"Go on now, ma'am."

On the other side of the glass, Ross could see passengers step onto the sand. Some sprinted toward the sea with flailing arms. Others stood still, clasping their bouquets, taking in their surroundings.

"What about you?" she asked the steward. "Won't you come with?"

"I cannot. I have a job to do."

"Wouldn't you be even better at your job if you knew what it was like? How can you convince people to visit a beach you've never been to?"

The steward didn't have an answer.

"Come," said Ross. "Come feel the ocean."

The steward's eyes drifted toward the scene behind the glass. He reached into his chest pocket and pulled out a small photograph. Running his thumb over the surface, he grabbed the phone from the receiver.

"LAST CALL FOR CAPE TECCAN!"

Ross beamed as the steward slid open the glass doors. They took each other's hand, held their breaths, and leapt from the train. Sun-heated sand slid into Ross's shoes. She kicked them off and let her feet sink into the warmth. Then she made her way toward the sea.

She reached the shore's edge. The foam gave kisses to her toes as it turned the ground beneath her cool. Within the crowd splashing in the water, Ross could see a wisp of lavender flowing in the wind. And there she stood—the steward by her side— looking beyond what she knew, where all she could smell was the salt air.

The Underwater Circus

We put on shell brassieres and dab rouge on our lips. We rub rose oil on our legs and wriggle them into our fishtails. Then we dive into the water, surrounded by glass.

Beneath the blue, we keep our smiles until our cheeks hurt. We wave at faces on the other side as our lungs shrink from the cold. We hold our breaths and hold our desires. Then we dart to the surface to keep ourselves alive.

During the day, children press their hands and noses against the panes. Delighted squeals are muted behind the walls of our stage. Little girls dream of growing up and becoming us. At night, their fathers show their tongues and make gestures of vulgarity born from drunkenness. We twist and turn and form circles with our bodies. When they see the flesh of our breasts in return for coins in their pockets, they hoot and howl. When our breasts reveal themselves beneath our coats outside liquor stores, they tell men with badges to take us away.

Some of us come home to empty houses. Some of us come home to husbands who refuse to ask about our day. Some of us go home with one another.

The first time we put on our fish tails, it becomes part of us until we are forced to let them go. Not many have reached this fate, but those who do never leave our memories.

Adelaide wanted more than anything to be one of us. She begged the ringmaster to give her a job, and he told her she looked homely and wasn't right for it. She filled her breasts with plastic to convince him and performed with us for a month before her chest turned red and splotchy. Adelaide's body had a bad reaction to the procedure. It needed to be undone or she would die.

When she returned from the hospital, we could see that her spirit had gone. She no longer greeted the tank with the fervor she once had. Her eyes were dim and weary. Eventually, Adelaide got hypothermia and replaced her tail with a wedding dress.

Marguerite met a cab driver at a hotel bar on her birthday. They said thirty words to each other and drank each other's whiskey. Marguerite had his child nine months later and could no longer squeeze into her tail. She cried and cried and begged the ringmaster to have a new one made. He let her go. Her crimson tail hung limply on top of the porpoise tank before they plucked a twenty-one-year-old from the crowd who could fit into it.

Josephine never wanted to be one of us. She had imagined herself in the main tank inside the ring. After one show, she'd approached the ringmaster and claimed she could ride sea turtles by placing her feet on two of their backs.

"Let me join your troupe," she'd begged. "You could use another balancing act."

The ringmaster made his decision with one glance at her ebony skin.

"A girl like you don't belong in the ring," he'd said. "Leave it to the twiggy men and muscled broads. I got another tank for ya."

He led her behind the curtain marked with the "$5" sign. She'd gasped at the sight of us.

"They're beautiful," she whispered. "Are they real?"

"Of course they're real," said the ringmaster. "And you're going to be one of them."

"Oh, I don't know," said Josephine. "I'd much rather join the acrobats. I'm good with animals."

"You can just as well be an acrobat in here," the ringmaster pressed. "My girls do as many tricks as the main performers. They just do them behind another pair of closed curtains."

Josephine understood the ringmaster wasn't going to give her a job unless she joined us. She agreed with the hope of proving herself worthy of the ring as time went on. We'd see her acting friendly with the elephant seal trainers between her shifts, spitting facts about the barking creatures they worked with as she petted their trunk-like noses. But we knew her efforts were in vain. The ringmaster had been searching for a dark-skinned belle. Now that he had her, he would never let her go.

We were all stunned when Josephine had her last day. It turned out she'd learned from the boy who cleans our tank that she was making two dollars less than the rest of us. When she confronted the ringmaster, he'd denied it and deducted a dollar from her wages for making such an accusation. So, she left her sunshine yellow tail behind. But no one could argue that she hadn't been forced to.

Josephine got a job cleaning the leopard cages at the zoo. It meant she could work in a place where she was respected, even if the respect came from the four-legged.

Nova was more beautiful than any of us. Ever since she was six years old, people would comment on her allure.

"Oh, her lips," they'd remark. "They're heart-shaped. And those eyes—those olive eyes!"

A young Nova would grin and bat her lashes and give a twirl to show off her dress.

Her beauty formed her. To Nova, it was the reason others wanted her around. It filled her stomach and got her gifts. It made people listen and gave her worth. It made it impossible for anyone to become angry with her.

We went to Nova's town when she was eighteen. She learned about us from the paperman.

"It's no ordinary circus," he'd exclaimed with wide eyes. "There's a giant tank inside the ring, as high as the tent itself."

"You mean to tell me," said Nova, "that the tent sitting in the middle of Kellerman Field has a giant water tank inside it?"

"That's what I said," replied the paperman.

"Where do I buy a ticket?"

Nova nearly sprained her neck staring up at the banner outside our tent for so long.

A SHOW THAT'LL HAVE YOU HOLDING YOUR BREATH!

Inside, she watched in awe as costumed high divers, clown-faced swimmers, and sea mammals swirled in the tank in front of her. Elephant seals waded through hoops. Turtles paddled in formation. Performers hung on to the fins of porpoises as they crashed in and out of the water. An octopus juggled an urchin shell.

She almost missed the sapphire curtain on the side of the tent. She wouldn't have known there was something behind it if she hadn't noticed the two schoolboys clutching candy apples darting into it.

Nova followed them. As soon as she saw the lively kaleidoscope of fish tails, she decided she'd found her new home.

"Mother," she announced to her poor old lady later that night. "I know what I am to be."

Nova's mother wanted her to become a seamstress and marry a decent man.

"I don't want to be loved by one man," said Nova. "I want to be admired by all of them."

She ran away with us and became the star of our show.

Whenever Nova was in the water, all eyes would be on the lines of her waist, the curves of her hips. We never envied her. The star always stayed in the tank longest. We made more money on nights Nova worked. She held on to the spotlight for over a decade. Everyone knew Nova the Sea Nymph.

The fear happened gradually. First, the ringmaster would bring in some bright-eyed teen who had just as much hope and conviction as she had back then. Soon, lines formed at the back of Nova's hands. A subtle darkness appeared beneath her eyes. Her hair got thinner. She breathed more heavily squeezing into her tail.

And then it happened all at once—the way the ocean kisses the shore a few times before crashing into it.

One day, as she was doing her usual flip turn, we saw Nova clutch her heart. She flailed her arms and launched herself to the surface as we pulled her out of the tank.

We asked her what was wrong, but she could only gasp to catch her breath.

The doctor attributed it to aging. Her body couldn't handle the water like it used to. She wasn't in her twenties anymore, he'd remarked.

Nova lied to the ringmaster at first. She assured him she was simply under the weather. But the ringmaster didn't like betting on people. He only bet on things.

"I can't have you ruining a show by choking in my tank," he told her.

"Please," Nova begged. "I'm the star."

And yet, to the ringmaster, she had no life in her left when it came to his business.

All throughout the night, we heard Nova sob over her vanity table. And as she looked up into the mirror and gazed beyond the heart-shaped lips and olive eyes, we could have sworn we heard her whisper.

"What am I if not this?"

The ringmaster must have had some sort of heart after all. When morning came, he strutted over to Nova with a sewing machine beneath one arm and placed it on her vanity.

"Tell you what," he said. "You keep the holes and frays outta these tails, and I'll pay ya weekly for it."

He kept his word. And Nova became a seamstress just like her mother always wanted.

That's how Nova came to be Mama.

"Hello, Mama," we'd chime.

"Hello, lovelies," she'd say, spinning the flywheel of her machine. Then she'd hand us our tails one by one and pass around the rose oil.

Mama watched every single one of our performances. When the moon made its presence known, she would put on men's clothing and blend in with the lawless crowd. She gave us notes on our somersaults.

"Don't stiffen your arms," she'd remind us. "Keep your fingers bent back."

She taught us how to tame the spectators—how to wink at them, how to shake our heads in a way that would make them amused rather than angry. She taught us everything she knew, for it kept her from withering.

Yet the more involved Mama became, the more difficult the ringmaster got. He'd open his mouth only to critique our performances. He'd snap if we strolled in a minute late or shut down our chatter with insults. He'd snatch bread rolls from our hands at supper, insisting they'd make us too bloated for the show. We could never tell which version of him we'd get until it was too late.

On a drizzly Saturday, we worked a late evening for a usual lot of unruly men and their coin-filled pockets. It wasn't long before one of them had enough drinks to begin pressing his pelvis against the tank. Though we were used to such manners, that night was different. The ringmaster had made us fast for days, and we were ravenous.

The youngest of us, Phoebe, was at the front of the tank. She was only seventeen—luscious lashes, a tail of orange damselfish. She'd only been with us for two weeks. The ringmaster had found her swiping liquor at a wedding she was never invited to.

Dear Phoebe had no mother or father. She was combative, hardly the type to turn a blind eye to a drunk showing her his jewels. Before we could grasp her arms, Phoebe put her face right up to the glass and flipped the bird.

The drunk responded by pounding his fist against the pane, rattling the sound within. It rang in our ears, and we no longer held our civility. Instead, we found ourselves emulating Phoebe—a ludicrous row of birds stretching across the tank. The most brazen of us did a few twirls before our one-finger salute.

The men shouted, spewing saliva in every direction, and demanded their money back. Mama ran to fetch the ringmaster, fearing for our well-being, but he cared only for the crowd's satisfaction. He assured them they'd be allowed back, free of charge. He even offered them more drinks, and a dance to close the night—from Nova the Sea Nymph herself.

Mama refused. She hadn't been in the tank for years.

"I should have tossed you to the streets," the ringmaster spat at her.

Outside, the drizzle turned to pouring rain that kept the men from leaving. They continued to make demands, their bellows growing more and more belligerent from the extra booze. We hurried to the surface as they pounded their fists against the glass. We were afraid to leave the tank, for the water was our only shield.

The ringmaster threatened to reveal Mama's disguise if she didn't perform.

"Imagine what they would do," he told her, "if they were made aware of a woman in this room."

He reached for her hat. We stayed at the surface, gripping the edge. The tank rattled, thunder boomed, and men roared. We felt the drums within our rib cages.

Then, as we peered over to the commotion below us, we saw the ringmaster clutch his heart. A doctor might have attributed it to aging, but some of us insist we saw her do it in the white of the lightning that burned through the tent.

He dropped to the ground. The crowd hollered and scattered, their cries dissipating across the field and into the night. We'd never seen drunks run so fast.

She looked up at us—the ringmaster at her feet—and there was no sound save the rain thrashing against the tent, the moans of the elephant seals. We released our holds on the edge of the tank, slowly and freely.

When we exist for them, they call us mermaids. When we live for ourselves, they call us sirens.

For thirty-one days, the curtains of our home remained shut. And when the show reopened, we were treated differently. Men no longer emptied their pockets. They didn't like that the new ringmaster was a woman.

For us, she still went by Mama.

"Hello, Mama," we'd chime.

"Hello, lovelies," she'd say.

We never dared ask her what happened that night. Neither did the acrobats, nor the animal trainers. We all feared that the mere mention would bring him back. And though he was gone, we found ourselves tossing biscuits in the trash after taking a bite.

During the day, little girls come in costumes to look like us. At night, their mothers come in beaded dresses, clutches in one hand and cocktails in the other. They dance and press their mouths against the glass. We blow kisses back and dart to the surface to keep ourselves alive.

And in the winter, when our bodies yearn to stay beneath the covers of our creaky beds, we place our feet on bitter wooden floors and wrap shawls around our frames. We put on shell brassieres and dab rouge on our lips. We rub rose oil on our legs and slip into our tails. Then we prepare our nerves for the cold.

Sage in Security

"**S**o, how long have you been green?"

Mr. Gatwidth wipes coffee from his 'stache with the back of his hand.

"Well, I assisted a developer while I was in college. Then I worked for a green start-up after graduating."

There's a loose thread on the sleeve of the mint cardigan I borrowed from my neighbor Anney. I'd needed something basic for an interview—something safer than the pleather jackets and shoulder-padded blazers I owned.

Anney had snorted when I slipped on the cardigan.

God, you look boring. But like, the kind of boring that people hire.

Why did she own this thing, anyway?

My mother bought it. You can keep it.

I'd pinned my hair up and added one of my favorite pairs of earrings. Maybe the dangling kaleidoscopic shapes would provide enough spunk that I wouldn't be forgettable.

Mr. Gatwidth leans back in his chair as he opens the wrapper of a candy bar.

"Want a piece?"

"Oh. No, thank you."

He takes a bite.

"As you know, the work we do here has been green for decades, along with the people. Not all green people can get their foot in the door, so you'd be lucky to be here."

"Yes. I'm very grateful to be considered. I'd like to show you the past projects that I've—"

"What kind of movies do you like?"

"I'm sorry?"

"Movies. What do you like to watch? We're all about movies in this office. We go out and see one together every Tuesday night."

"Oh. I'm not much of a—well, no, that's fine."

"Good, good. You were saying something?"

"I—"

"Your past projects?"

"Yes. I'd like to show you my portfolio, if you don't mind." I turn the book toward him. "It'd give you an idea of what I can do."

Mr. Gatwidth licks his thumb and flips through the pages, dampening the corners with saliva laced with chocolate. He scans the details of each program I created. The silence kills me, so I fill it.

"That's a software I designed to secure the company's digital assets. And that's a code I wrote to—"

"Yes, this would work." He slams the book shut. "Here's what we'll do. Thirty hours a week, at twenty-nine rollads an hour. If you start at that for a while, I think you'd have a very bright future here."

I try not to move my face. Twenty-nine rollads is even more than I hoped for. Is this the pay at all green corporations? I can't believe my luck.

Mr. Gatwidth takes out a contract from his desk drawer, pushes it toward me, and shoves the rest of the candy bar into his mouth. He points to where I'm meant to sign. I stare at the chocolate fingerprint on the paper.

"Sorry, can I have a moment to read—"

"Of course, of course. It's just the usual la-dee-la. Don't steal our things. Don't touch people's bums. Don't blow up the building if yer fired for touching people's bums."

"Right."

I sign on the contract, marked with faded cyan and yellow lines as the result of a printer out of ink.

"You'll be working at the Sage level with all the IT and security members on this floor." He opens his desk drawer and slides a sage-colored card to me.

"When you arrive on Monday, scan this in the elevator. Press three for the fourth floor, where we are now. If you press four, it's really the fifth, where the Emerald offices are, and you won't be able to get in."

He chokes on a piece of chocolate and coughs. After pounding his chest with his fist, he continues.

"Limes are on two, which you're welcome to visit during your break. They have table tennis. Viridians are on one. They'll help you grab supplies if you need anything for your desk. G is the ground floor, and the O button is for the Olive level."

He licks his fingers. "You won't need to go there."

I only ever worked as a Viridian at my last job. So many long, monotonous days answering phones, entering data, stringing together paperclips into chains long enough to hang myself with. Once in a while, a Sage member would come down to pick up their mail and ramble about whatever issue they were trying to solve. I don't think they ever expected me to process anything they said. Maybe that's why they trusted me.

You gotta think like the hacker, they'd say, *Get in their heads. That's how you stop them.* As if hackers and serial killers were one and the same.

I'd do my best to pull information out of them, getting tastes of sweet-smelling sage and poking for details on walls they were hitting. They loved to rant, so that part was easy. I'd go home, stay up late downing cups of matcha, and churn out pieces of code. Convincing them to take a look at my work was the hard part, but after spending weeks trying to solve something with no luck, they'd bite. Not everything in my portfolio actually came to fruition, but our sweet-toothed friend doesn't need to know that.

"Welcome to the team," says Mr. Gatwidth.

I thank him profusely as I stand, my portfolio pressed against my chest.

"Wait," he calls as I head toward the door. I turn to find a chocolate bar being extended to me. "Little treat to celebrate!"

"Oh," I say, taking it awkwardly. "Thanks."

I slip the portfolio and the chocolate into my bag. Mr. Gatwidth never gets up from his chair.

I'm thankful for the moment alone inside the elevator. I stare at the keycard between my fingers. It almost glows.

As I exit through the revolving glass doors, the guard tips his hat.

"I'll be seeing you again," I say to him. "I work here now."

"Wonderful, miss! What department?"

"Security."

"Ah. You and I both."

I pause, confused. He chuckles.

"It's a joke. See?" He points to his uniform.

"Oh! Right. Yes."

The city makes its usual noise, but I can only focus on the wondrous sound of my heels clicking upon pavement. The trees look especially lush. Everything in my path is greener.

When I get to my building, Anney's on the front steps smoking half a cigarette she'd hidden in a planter box.

"How do those not get wet?" I ask.

"Nobody waters succulents. How'd the interview go?"

"Good. I got the job."

"Shut the fuck up."

"I start Monday."

"Lucky fucking cardigan."

The butt dies beneath her gold Chelsea boot. There's a run in her tights from knee to thigh. I follow her inside our tiny vestibule lined with mailboxes beneath a dim hanging bulb. She pulls out her keys and opens Number 24. It's empty.

"Goddammit. They're taking forever to send my check."

"For the mural on Tuscany Street?"

"Yeah. Bastards. I need new brushes."

It takes almost all of Anney's strength for her to push the heavy glass door that opens to the lobby. The run-down elevator smells of chemicals and urine. We yank the necks of our shirts over our noses, and I use my knuckle to press the cracked plastic button to our floor.

"Are you going to move apartments?" Anney asks, her voice muffled behind her oversized T-shirt. "Now that you can afford to get out of this shithole?"

"Of course not," I assure her. "The office is a walk away. It's that giant building next to the juice bar you like."

The elevator doors open, and we breathe again.

"Hey," I say as we shuffle down the hall. "Do you think Jonah can take a look at my shower this weekend? The water's weak. I'll buy him that bourbon he likes."

"Sure thing."

Jonah is a guy Anney's been dating for nine months that she won't admit is her boyfriend. I know it's because her mother wouldn't be pleased with her daughter dating someone in the brown industry. He and Anney met when our landlord sent out a maintenance crew to fix her fridge. Her mother always pushed her to date among the Burgundy level, like a psychiatrist or a surgeon, but at this point she'd settle for any nurse or teacher in the red field.

And then there are those like Anney who work yellow—artists, freelancers, musicians constantly seeking gigs for their next paycheck. If they've yet to lose hope, they're my favorite kind of people. But there's a certain point they get to that can be devastating to be around. Anney weaves in and out of both. Maybe it's the duality that makes me care for her.

She reaches her door, and I reach mine.

"Keep a lookout for Lime openings at your company, okay?"

Her request surprises me. "You sure you'd want a nine-to-five?"

"For the Lime level, I'd do it. That's the dream. You get to be green without losing your yellow." She unlocks her door. "You want some cornbread? I made it this morning."

"I'm okay. I'm gonna go make lunch. I'll see you."

"See ya, Miss Fancy Analyst."

"Good morning, team! Say hello to our new analyst, Deja."

Mr. Gatwidth stands me in front of ten apathetic faces behind desks like it's my first day of kindergarten.

"Oh," I say. "Actually, my na—"

"Mr. Kitto, why don't you show her where the coffee is? Then make sure she's all set up."

A guy about my age raises two fingers to his forehead in a salute. His pullover is a little too short for his above-average height, revealing striped boxers peeking out of his loose khakis.

"Right on. Sup, Deja. Follow ya boy, Clad."

The Sage-level floor is filled with offices and conference rooms encased in glass. I hadn't thought about it at the interview, but it's an ironic choice for a security team. We pass by clear boxes of men sitting in front of computers, screens lighting their faces green. For a moment, I get a sinking feeling in my chest.

"Members looking out for AFGAs sit together," Clad remarks.

"Right," I say, making a mental note to look up what AFGA stands for.

We reach the doorless break room, also made of glass. An island of machines and energy bars sits in the center.

"Decaf?"

"Regular."

"How much cream?"

"None. Thanks."

Clad scrunches his brows as he hands me the temperature-control mug. I let the smoky aroma hover beneath my nose as I follow him back down the hall.

"So," he says, "I'm sure Big G has given you the rundown, but we're going to put you on an issue we received last week."

I have no idea what Clad's referring to, but I do my best to play it off. "Sure, yeah. He didn't really give details, though."

"A company claims one of their VCs had his computer hacked. Passwords to his email accounts were compromised. Seems basic, but the same thing happened to another member of their company on the same weekend. They're worried it's no coincidence."

"Huh. And their bank accounts?"

"They froze them before anyone could get to them. And we've already looked into whether the attack came from inside."

"So . . . it didn't?"

"They're one of the biggest firms in the world. Their firewall has more rules than my mother on a Sunday. Of course it didn't."

As we reach our own glass box, Clad leads me to an empty desk.

"This is you, next to Laeon."

Laeon has massive headphones over his beanie and a half-eaten breakfast burrito leaning against his monitor. He doesn't look at me. Neither do any of the other guys.

I set the coffee down on my desk. Clad opens its drawer and pulls out some folders.

"These are their employee files and reports detailing the issue. They asked each of them to provide a list of their locations that week."

He pulls keys from his pocket and gives them a playful toss in the air before catching them in his palm. Then he unlocks the filing cabinet in the corner of the room and takes out two laptops.

"Here are their computers. Let me know when you take lunch, and I'll lock them up."

"Can I take these home with me at the end of the day? The files, I mean."

Clad gives me the same look he did when I asked for black coffee. For a moment, the only sound is the click-clacking of typing at other desks.

"Knock yourself out. I'll be downstairs testing the new game the Limes designed. Laeon will answer your questions." Even after he disappears, his department store body spray lingers.

I take a seat in the swivel chair as Laeon strips off his headphones.

"I can't stand him," he says.

"Oh. Yeah. I get that."

He points to the sticky note on the mousepad.

"That's your login. You'll want to fill out the onboarding documents at the link."

"Cool. Thanks."

"There's a ton. I doubt you'll get to that assignment today."

"Right."

As I scroll through the company's internal system, I notice it's scrambling some words. It'll say things like "Payroll and miTe Cards" or "Complete skaT."

"Hey, uh, it looks like the system is doing this thing—"

"Ah, yeah. It's a stupid bug." Laeon picks up the burrito and peels back the foil.

"Why hasn't it been fixed?" I ask.

"Keeps getting pushed. Gatwidth says there are 'bigger bugs to swat.' Ugh . . . I can't stand cilantro." He takes a bite anyway.

The computer gives me a loading bar. As I wait, I examine the files in the first folder.

"Let's see . . . what's special about this guy?"

"Nothing," Laeon comments with his mouth full. "They're all the same."

I open the other folder, scanning information on the other member who was hacked.

"That's strange," I say. "She's Pewter level. Works in their HR Department."

"So?"

"Why would someone want to get into a Pewter's device?"

"All grays have something to hide. Bunch of rapacious rats. I can't stand them."

Laeon slips his headphones back on. The computer finishes loading the page. I make a mental note to look up "rapacious."

Ada licks my face.

"I missed you too, girl, but you gotta get off me!"

I toss my keys onto the counter along with a plastic bag of brushes I bought from the art supply store on the way home. I'd give those to Anney in the morning. At the moment, all I want to do is eat a supermarket cucumber roll and solve a mystery.

Ada sticks her long Manchester terrier nose into my work bag as I drop it onto the couch. I shoo her away, reach into it, and take out the folders. Fumbling through them, I pull the pages listing the members' whereabouts the week of the cyberattack. The pages come with me to the fridge as I retrieve my dinner. I scan the VC's list first, reading names of restaurants, office buildings, and gyms. *Gyms.* Plural. Who goes to two gyms?

I put the pages side by side on my kitchen island, then rip open a soy sauce packet with my teeth. Ada paws at me, and I toss her a piece of the roll before drizzling the sauce over the rest.

None of the locations from either member match each other. I'd figured that much. But there has to be a connection somewhere.

I pick a random cafe on the HR employee's list. When I enter it into my phone, I notice that it's thirty miles outside the city. My thumb hits the menu by accident. Eight rollads for a macchiato? Sheesh. No wonder Laeon hates these people.

There's a knock at the door. Sigh. I hate being interrupted when I'm eating.

It's a delivery guy with a package. Ada provides her usual excessive noise when she sees him.

"Sorry," I say as I yank her collar. "She barks at new faces. *Sit!*"

He holds out a clipboard for me to sign, and I take the box. It's from my parents.

When he leaves, I rip open the package and read the note.

Found on our trip. Love you.

There's an expensive bottle of champagne along with toiletries from the hotel. Travel gifts are the only times I ever see their money.

I sniff the tissue-wrapped bar soap before getting back to work. The champagne will have to wait.

Another piece of sushi goes into my mouth as I continue scrolling through the cafe's website. A piece of cucumber falls onto the floor. Ada is grateful.

It's possible the device was compromised using the cafe's network, though it's hard to believe someone in HR would need a computer outside of work. It's also possible she logged into the network on her phone. But that would mean the VC's issue is a coincidence after all, which is even harder to believe.

One by one, I type every location on the VC's list into the search bar on my phone. Nothing stands out until I get close to the bottom of the page, where one of the gyms is listed.

A quick click tells me it's thirty miles outside of the city.

I stuff another piece into my mouth. As I stare off, pondering the coincidence I've discovered, the hotel toiletries on the other end of the kitchen island meet my line of sight.

I'm hit with wasabi.

I wake to Ada pawing at me for her morning walk. Sunlight pierces through the open blinds into my living room.

SHIT.

With my mind focused on the case and my stomach filled with three glasses of my parents' gift, I fell asleep on the couch and forgot to set an alarm. I grab my phone from the coffee table to check the time. It's twenty minutes past when I should have been up.

When I dash into my bathroom, however, I realize that tardiness is the least of my problems.

The mirror above the sink almost laughs as I clutch its sides in a panic. My hair, usually bouncing with life, is now limp and oily. My eyes are a different color, my nose is no longer round, and my once-thin lips are now full. To put it frankly, I HAVE A COMPLETELY DIFFERENT FACE THAN I DID THE DAY BEFORE.

What the actual—no, no, no! This isn't happening.

I pinch my cheeks and yank at my ears as though they'd magically turn back to the way they were. No cigar. *Goddammit.*

I knock my knuckles against my forehead.

If I miss the second day of work, I'm toast.

Ada whines.

"Okay. Okay, okay," I say, gathering my thoughts. "Hang on, girl."

I fly down the hallway to Anney's. My fists pound on the door as I yell her name. No answer.

Dammit, Anney! I really needed you to have NOT spent the night at Jonah's today.

I rush back to my place. *Think, think, think.*

Could I pull off being a cousin of mine? I check my bedroom mirror again. Yes, I suppose I could. I could go into the office and say there's been some sort of family emergency, then leave my findings on Clad's desk, as much as that pains me. I'd just have to figure out how to bypass the security guard at the front.

Ada paces back and forth as I peel off yesterday's clothes. I slip on jeans and a knitted sweater. It isn't what I'd normally wear to work, but I'm not me today, am I?

"All right. Come on, girl. Quick walk, okay?"

Minutes later, as my dog relieves herself beneath a sidewalk tree, I give Anney a ring.

She greets me with, "What up, bitch!"

"Hey, look, I don't have time to explain—I'm outside with Ada and I'm late, so I gotta go. Can you do me a favor and give her a proper walk when you get back? You have the spare key, right?"

"You're never late for anything," Anney says. "What's up?"

"Nothing! I just forgot to set an alarm."

"I don't believe you."

"Anney, can you please just freaking—"

"Oh my gawd, chill. I'll walk your damn dog."

I sigh. "There's something on the counter for you. In the plastic bag."

"It better not be your bullshit." She hangs up.

I toss a full poop bag into a nearby trash bin and force a disappointed Ada back up the steps into the building.

The security guard scarfs down the last piece of his bagel when he sees me. I clear my throat, preparing my lie in my head, praying he'll let me into the office.

"Hi, there," I attempt in my sweetest voice. "How are you? I'm—"

"Running late today, miss? Better get up there!"

He . . . recognizes me? I shuffle inside, words escaping me. Could it be that the face I've obtained belongs to someone else who works here?

I pull my elevator card from my bag and scan it before pressing 3. The double doors close, and though I'm alone, the blurred reflection of a stranger in the steel walls stares back at me. The lift hums its way up, and I notice something off about the card in my hand. It appears less green than it did before. It's almost . . . olive?

Stop. You're losing your mind.

Clad's standing in front of the elevator when it opens. I jump when I see him. My heart throws itself out of my chest as he stares at me with a squint. I've been busted. He can see my new face—I'm sure of it.

"Tardiness isn't a good color on you." He rests an arm against one of the doors to keep them from closing. "Lucky for you, Big G's out today. I won't tell, if you buy lunch."

He . . . doesn't see it? My tongue goes dry as I try to come up with something to steer the conversation.

Clad stands there with a smirk that I have a desperate desire to break.

"I finished the assignment," I spout.

It works. The smirk breaks. I step forward, and he lets me out.

"Not completely," I add. "But I'm close."

Clad scoffs. "Well, I'm sure the team will be *thrilled* to hear what you think you know. Weekly meeting's in five minutes."

There's a weekly meeting? Why does nobody tell me anything?

When I reach our glass box, I could swear Laeon shows an ounce of excitement. By "excitement," I mean his shoulders are an inch less slouched than they were before.

"Thought you'd quit," he mumbles. He has an egg sandwich this time. There are three abandoned pieces of avocado on his plate.

I sit beside him, relieved he doesn't notice my new face either. "Let me guess. You can't stand avocado?"

"Allergic."

The other guys start pushing back their chairs. A few give me quick nods as they pass us on their way to the door. Some, I didn't see the day before. I wonder whether they're meeting me for the first time with a face that isn't mine.

Laeon yawns and stretches his arms before getting up. "I can't stand these meetings."

I grab my bag and follow the team to the conference room. If the guard, Clad, *and* Laeon recognize me, surely no one else will notice anything different, right?

We sit ourselves down in the conference room, which is basically just a bigger glass box with a long table in the center. Clad strolls in four minutes late, plopping down into the seat at the head of it.

"Goooood morning, associates," he partly sings. "Glenn, hit us with the agenda this week."

A guy who looks half my age clears his throat. "I'm hoping we can work on our system update. I've been trying to push this, but other projects keep getting prioritized."

Clad slides a strip of gum into his mouth. "Right, right. We'll start soon."

"We had members leave last month," Glenn presses. "And . . . not on great terms. I'm not comfortable with our current firewalls. Besides, our system has a ridiculous bug. It's scrambling both letters and numbers. A Viridian bought me a cake because the birthdate on my employee form said 10/21 instead of 12/10."

"So, you got an early cake! What's the big deal?" Clad scoffs. "Relax, Glenn. There aren't going to be any AFGAs."

I forgot to look up that damn acronym. The faint reflection of my new face taunts me from the glass wall in front of me. I turn to Laeon.

"Hey," I whisper. "What's AFGA?"

Laeon rolls his eyes. "He's the only one that calls them that. It stands for Attacks from Former Green Agents. The rest of us just call them green threats."

"Ah! Since Deja's ready to talk," Clad interjects, "let's move on to out-of-house projects. Care to share what you found?"

All eyes are on me. I have a sudden desperation to bury my head inside the garbage bin behind Clad. Someone is bound to spot the differences in my face now.

Laeon nudges me.

"R-right!" I stammer, pulling the files from my bag and shuffling them onto the table. "The issue we received from the VC . . . I was, um, examining the list of locations provided. The other member of the company visited a cafe just half a mile away from a gym he went to."

Clad lets out a breath. "So?"

"I just—both those places are thirty miles away, so I thought that was kind of strange. I mean, two people from the same company visit a random town outside the city on the same weekend?"

"People go on weekend trips," Clad says. "What's the big deal?"

My tongue is dry again. "Well, um, the thing is . . . they visited those places on Saturday *and* Sunday. It's unlikely they'd both make trips that far from where they live two days in a row. They must've had to spend the night at a hotel. I believe they intentionally left this location off the list."

"Because they want to make our jobs harder?" Clad pops his gum.

I pull my hair in front of my face, hiding my mouth behind it. "Well, why would two people not want their company knowing they spent the night at the same hotel? They're most likely in a relationship . . . an affair."

The other guys perk up as Clad leans his chair back, rocking back and forth. My anxiety doesn't let him respond.

"Anyway," I continue, "I did a search, and there's only one hotel in that town. Well, there's also a run-down motel, but a VC would have the cash to splurge. I could be wrong, but my gut says the hotel is where they were hacked."

"Impossible," Clad responds, still rocking. "Their computers have systems that protect them from public networks. It's a venture capital firm. They're not idiots."

"I get that. But there is another way. It's possible they weren't logged into the hotel Wi-Fi at all, but only thought they were."

I reach into my bag and take out a hacker's cheat sheet I'd secretly made a copy of at my last job.

Laeon helps me pass it down. It slides through a few guys' hands before reaching Clad.

"There are programmers who create networks," I explain, "that appear as something else. In this case, they might name the network after the hotel so that anyone who sees it assumes it's the right one. They make the login password the same, but really, you're logging into their network and giving them access to your information."

Laeon lets out a whistle.

"So, they don't really have it out for anyone specific. They just wait for whoever logs into their network and get what they can. In this case, they lucked out with the VC. The woman from HR was just, well, collateral damage."

I press my bag against my chest as though it might silence the thumping inside it.

"My suggestion," I conclude, "is to tell them that as long as they've changed their passwords and frozen their accounts, they have nothing left to worry about. Their information can only be stolen when they use that network. We simply need to block it and let the hotel know about the issue."

My stomach starts eating at itself. I'd forgotten breakfast.

"Dude," Laeon says with something like astonishment. "You just solved that without even looking at the devices."

Clad lets his chair meet the ground again and removes his feet from the table. "No one's solved anything. We won't know if the theory's correct until we check the devices." He stands. "Glenn, get on it."

Glenn furrows his brow. "Shouldn't she be the one to—"

"An experienced team member should handle the rest," Clad replies as he exits the room.

I bite my tongue. *Same shit, different face.*

After stuffing myself with four granola bars from the break room, I return to the office to find the guys hovering around a laptop.

"Yo, Deja! You were right!" one shouts at me.

I sigh. "It's not D—"

"I was blocking the network on the devices," Glenn exclaims. "Sorry. Clad asked me. Anyway, we did a little digging, and . . ."

He turns the computer toward me. "We found this photo in one of his folders. It's Mister VC and Miss HR looking pretty close."

"Oh, wow," I reply. "We probably shouldn't be looking at this . . ."

"That's not it," Glenn continues. "We did an online search for the guy, and turns out his wife is a partner of their firm. Makes sense why he'd go through such lengths to hide the affair. Anyway . . ."

He shuts down the device. "Clad seemed a little put off by the whole thing. I think he left to hang out with the Limes again."

"I swear, they're paying him fifty rollads to do absolutely nothing," Laeon grumbles.

"Fi-*fifty* rollads?" I ask. "How do you know that?"

"Oh, he's not secretive about it at all," Glenn chimes in. "Quite the opposite."

Suddenly, my twenty-nine rollads doesn't feel so great anymore.

"E-excuse me," I stammer. "Gotta use the . . . yeah."

I rush out and weave through the halls of endless glass boxes to the bathrooms, eyeing the sign with the dress-wearing stick figure.

Stumbling over my own feet, I use all my body weight to push open the heavy squeaking door. I receive my moment of peace as it closes behind me and I stare at the empty lavatory, stalls all cracked open and green music warbling through speakers in the ceiling.

I walk toward one of the mirrors above a sink, and the reflection that stares back has little spunk. The eyes appear tired and lost, doubtful. They're yellow or red or brown, but they aren't mine.

Who are you?

The fear I had when this new face first ambushed me dissipates into sadness, and I press my tongue to the roof of my mouth to stop myself from crying. *Not at work. Never at work.*

I pull my phone from my pocket and dial.

"Yes, I walked your dog."

"Hey, Anney."

"What's up?"

I look into the mirror. "I don't know . . . something's going on. Something weird. I just—"

"It's your first day. You're freaking out. It'll pass."

"It's like I'm someone else. I can't help this feeling that I'm not supposed to be here."

I can hear Anney crunching on something on the other end. "Stop that. You deserve to be there just as much as any one of those green dweebs."

"What if they hired me because they needed to fill a quota or something?"

"Good!" Anney blurts through her munching. "Maybe they'll learn something for once."

When I don't answer, Anney stops eating whatever snack she has.

"Look, you goof," she says to me. "We've lived in the same building for three years. You've been green for as long as I've known you. At the theme park, you described your idea for an entire encryption software to me on a dive coaster."

I laugh. "Thanks, Anney."

"I'll see ya later, okay? You got this."

"What are you eating?"

"Potato chips."

She hangs up.

The squeak of the door startles me as a woman enters.

"Oh. Hi there," she greets me.

"H-hi."

I haven't seen another woman on the Sage level before. She looks older than I am, but not more than ten years. Her lips are painted black, contrasting the white pencil dress clinging to her curves. A green ribbon holds up the bun in her hair. I feel a sudden embarrassment over my jeans as her oxford heels click across the floor.

She runs the water from the sink beside me.

"I always think pomegranate is a good idea," she laughs. "And end up scrubbing my hands."

"Do—do you work on this floor?" I ask.

"Yeah. Data scientist. You?"

"Security analyst."

"Right on." She yanks a towel from the wall and dries her hands. "Glad I can share the bathroom with somebody for once."

Her wit gives me sudden courage, and I blurt out, "Do you ever question whether you belong here?"

She laughs again before tossing the towel into the trash.

"Of course," she says. "But it only gets in the way. The point is, I am here. And I can spend my time proving them right or proving them wrong."

She reaches the door and yanks the handle with ease.

"Let yourself breathe," she adds. "If you don't, they'll see what you see."

Clad doesn't return to the office until the end of the day. When he does, Glenn gives him the rundown of the day's work, including informing the hotel about the suspicious network.

"Good," Clad says, spinning in his chair. He stops when it's turned toward me. "Huh. Did you change your hair or something?"

I gulp. "What? No."

"There's something off about you."

"Really? Weird. I . . . didn't change anything."

I look away from him and focus on my computer screen. He drags his feet across the floor and rolls his chair over to my desk.

"No," he decides. "There's definitely something different about your face."

I frantically begin closing windows and attempt to shut down my computer. It begins an update instead. *Really? Now? Can you just let me go home?*

"Yeah, I'm sure of it," Clad presses. "Big G hires you out of nowhere, we give you an assignment, and you solve it overnight? Something's off about you."

My blood begins to boil. It's one thing to question my own abilities, but to have someone *else* question them? Someone like Clad, of all people?

The computer continues showing its yellow spinning wheel on a blue screen.

You've been green for as long as I've known you.

I turn to Clad. "You pass assignments on to us and spend the rest of your day with the Limes. Maybe something's off about *you*."

"Oh, shit," Laeon whispers. The other guys look at the floor as they slip on their jackets.

The corner of Clad's mouth twitches. I have no idea whether he has the power to fire me.

He rolls his chair back to his desk. "It's Tuesday," he says. "Come with us to the movies."

"S-sure," I reply.

The update on my computer finishes, and as the screen goes from blue to black, I recognize the reflection looking back at me.

"Wait," I say.

Clad turns around.

"About the system update . . ." I tell him. "We need to get the team on that sooner. I know you said next week, but—"

"We have one of the strongest security systems in the nation."

"We use keycards to get into the elevator."

Laeon snorts. Glenn hides a smile.

"Fine," Clad says. "We'll start tomorrow." He slips on his sweatshirt and leaves our box, zigzagging through labyrinthine glass.

As the rest of us follow him, Laeon puts his mouth beside my ear. "You didn't hear from me, but someone told me he's Gatwidth's nephew."

"Everything makes sense now."

"Yup."

The entire team squeezes into the fancy elevator, shoulders touching. It smells of steel and obnoxious cologne.

Clad nudges my arm. "Wanna scan us down?"

I pull my keycard from my bag, remembering its change in color. Before I can hide it from the others, Glenn peers over my shoulder.

"Looks like you got chocolate on it," he says, reaching over and rubbing it off with his thumb. "Did the boss give you one of his awful candy bars? Those things melt like crazy."

I peek inside my bag. "Dammit. You're right."

I scan the card, and we descend. When we reach the ground floor, we all spill out, stumbling over each other. The security guard gives a chuckle. He tips his hat as he passes us. "Have a wonderful evening," he says, entering the elevator.

I turn around at the *ding!* and watch as the floor designator goes from G to O.

We exit the building. A familiar face runs up to me.

"Ugh, finally! The guard wouldn't let me smoke out here. What's the point of having a phone if you put it on silent? I've been calling you forever!"

"Anney, what are you—"

"You were such a bummer earlier, I wasn't going to *not* check on you. Anyway, you said it was the building by the juice parlor. I'm here so we can get those stupid thoughts outta you over dinner."

"She can't," Clad remarks. "We're going to the movies."

Anney doesn't miss a beat. "Nobody asked you, dickhead."

I put my hand up as a signal for her to tone it down.

"I'll do movies next week," I assure the guys.

Clad boos. "Aw, come on. Don't be lame, Deja."

"Deja?" says Anney. "Who the fuck is that?"

I realize I never told her about the system's bug and the mix-up it's caused. The team stares at us, waiting for me to say something. On the other side of the street, a dive bar turns on its sign, casting a green glow across their blank faces.

I remove the melted chocolate bar from my bag and toss it into a trash bin.

"My name isn't Deja," I tell them, hooking my arm through Anney's. "It's Jade."

Deceased, Return to Sender

Dear Maggie,

I am sorry it's been so long since we last spoke. Perry's grown so quickly, and each year seems to bring more things to keep us busy. School plays, swimming, tutoring . . . he's even joined the ballet school with his sister. I don't recall having this many activities when I was a little girl, but they insist on them and whine when we miss an occasion. Anyway, you asked for photos of them last summer, so I've enclosed a few from their holiday recital inside the envelope.

A new radiator should be arriving at your home in the days after you receive this letter. They couldn't tell me why yours would be making that noise, but sleep is so important for one's health, and I figured you should receive a replacement. If you hear a knock at the door, ask who they are before opening it, and if they say anything about a radiator, do let them in so that they may install it. Everything's been paid for, so please don't hand them anything.

I suppose I've been doing fine, though I've become wearier myself. My body has grown heavy, and my steps feel cumbersome when I weave through our hallway to clean each room. I haven't gained any weight or anything like that. It's as though it's coming from inside me, or rather, put upon me by another being. Every day it pushes me toward the ground a tiny bit more—not enough that I can't take it, but it builds and swallows me slowly until it starts to reveal itself in strange, inconvenient ways.

Last month, I was lying in bed one morning long after the alarm had gone off when I heard music through the window. Someone in the building next to ours had turned on the radio in their kitchen. They started to do the dishes, the water gushing and porcelain rattling against the song. I stayed still, listening to the melody that consumed the air between our windows. Metallic strings tied our building to theirs, horns shook both our walls. It was not unlike Mozart's 29th. I couldn't bring myself to stop listening. It was as though someone had placed flour sacks over my hands and feet, forcing me to remain there. Have you ever been restrained by sound? I both enjoyed and despised the music. I enjoyed it enough to keep listening, but despised it for keeping me in bed. I could hear Hazel calling for me beneath the lullaby. We were running late for her dress rehearsal.

If Hiro were here, the children would never be late for anything. His promptness was one of the main reasons that I fell for him, along with his stoicism. I liked that he was quiet in a way where he didn't feel the need to talk big, but not too quiet that I'd have to exhaust myself filling the silence. Then we married and the children came, and they filled his heart so much that he became quieter and quieter and farther and farther until I sometimes could not remember his voice at all.

So when he died, I grieved much more for the children than I did for myself. They loved their father more than they could ever love me—I'd accepted that a long time ago. He was always more affectionate, warmer, more in tune with their needs. Even when Hazel was a baby, whenever she cried, he would know exactly whether she was hungry or sleepy or had soiled herself. I'd search frantically for her pacifier, assuming that was what she wanted, only to realize the wailing had ceased and he had successfully burped her.

Even when he was angry, the children lightened his mood in a way that I never could. I would try hard to get through to him (bring him tiramisu or cherry pie to cheer him up), but he'd grumble and walk away from me until Perry would run into the room, and he'd scoop him up in his arms and they'd sway together until they both giggled.

Sometimes I wonder whether my husband resented my nature. I love my children, I do, but not like other mothers who love their children. You know, the kinds that glisten and gleam and cut out tiny pictures to paste inside lockets. I used to envy how beautiful they looked whenever they spoke of their little ones.

Theodore has started banging on the piano keys, they'd say, and their eyes would well up with pride and their cheeks would turn rosy pink and their souls would sing high, euphonious notes that mine could never hit.

I tried as hard as I could during the first few years of Hazel's life. I did my best to blend in— baking cinnamon rolls for her peers, putting on rouge before lunches with the other mothers. I tried to talk about my child the way they spoke of theirs, but it would always lead to my rambling awkwardly over tiny things like the tangles in her hair. The more I tried, the more obvious it became that I wasn't like them until I decided not to pretend anymore for Hazel's sake. It was better for her to have a mother who never made an appearance than to have one that people whispered about. Eventually, she grew independent enough that it didn't matter, and by the time Perry came along, I stopped trying to mold myself into what I thought they needed and stopped wondering whether there was something wrong with me.

It's only when they look at me the way I used to look at you that I begin to mind. I'm sure you understand that by now and won't get offended by my saying so. I know you desperately wanted my love while I was growing up. I have love for you, of course, in the way anybody loves someone because they're bound by blood. But I don't love you the way you want me to, which is a love by choice. You know that and I know that, and now this must be my punishment, because now the children know that feeling all too well.

Anyway, I'm writing you this letter because our calls just won't seem to connect. I keep hearing the ringing when I dial your number until you say hello and I respond, but you continue to say hello as though you cannot hear me, so we hang up and sometimes you try to call back, then I would say hello myself only to receive silence. This has happened several times now, and the odd thing is, the calls don't show up in my records. I keep meaning to inform the telephone company of the issue, but it's been so busy with the children, and well, you know how that goes. Perhaps after they finish their courses this summer, we'll fly out for a week so you can meet them.

~~Sincerely,~~
~~Love,~~
~~All the best,~~
Your daughter,
Pearl

Sleep Crust

The first time Francis found a pie in her oven was the morning after she slept with the cable guy. Her network line had been chewed by a rat that her landlord had been ignoring for six months.

The pie was pecan. The guy was in her bathroom.

"Did you make this?" she asked him.

"What?" he said, shaking his hands dry as he came out. "No."

"Then who did?"

"How should I know?" He stumbled while putting on his cheap white sneakers. "I gotta leave for work. Thanks for the Chinese takeout."

The door swung itself shut behind him.

Francis stood there, bewildered. There were leftover pecans from a pasta recipe she had attempted weeks earlier, so she wandered over to them to see if they had been used. But as she stared into the half-empty bag, she couldn't even remember how much she had in the first place.

Had someone entered her apartment with a pie and left it in her oven with the light on for her to see? Had someone baked it in her kitchen? Had she somehow baked it herself in her sleep?

She opened the fridge to check the eggs, but again, she could not remember how many she'd had to begin with. Surely, if she had baked a pie in her sleep, there would be a mess left behind. The act of baking in one's sleep was already mind-boggling—she could not fathom having cleaned as well.

It *had* to have been the guy from the cable company. Yes, he was probably joking around. Although, making a pie was such a considerate thing to do, and that didn't really align with the type of lover he had been.

Francis placed the pie on the counter, turned off the oven light, and took a shower. She laid on the couch in her robe and scrolled on her phone for a while afterward. Eventually, she made herself a coffee.

As she watched the steam rise from the mug, she could not ignore the pie that sat beside it. Francis grabbed a spoon from the rusty dish rack beside the sink and plunged it into the dessert. She moaned when the caramel filling touched her tongue.

She took another bite. And another. With each delectable chunk washed down with coffee, Francis told herself to stop eating. But just as quickly as the pie had entered her life, it was gone.

Francis threw the round aluminum pan into the trash, empty except for crumbs. Then she maneuvered around the piles of things scattered on her floor toward the bedroom, where she picked up a raglan shirt from beneath her bed, put it on, and walked three blocks of the bustling metropolis to the deli where she worked.

While Francis tied an apron around herself, the owner, Mr. Do, complained about the floors.

"You no sweep! Never sweep!" he rattled. "Lettuce everywhere, all the time!"

"Sorry," Francis told him. "It's been busy here since Angelo's deli shut down."

"Then sweep after close!"

When she'd earned a degree in communications two years earlier, Francis had admitted she didn't know what she wanted for her career. But she definitely hadn't thought it would lead to a life of slapping together mediocre sandwiches six days a week. She had applied to every office job she could find in the city and finally given up after her thirty-second failed interview. Her godmother always told her she had an unlikable quality during a first impression.

"You act like people are wasting your time," she'd point out, "when you're the one that asked to be there."

That was certainly not the vibe Francis wanted to give off. She tried hard to counteract the unlikableness with comments like "Thank you so much for your time" or "I like the way you decorate," but it all came out sounding flat. The only occasions her demeanor seemed to work wonders was whenever someone wanted to sleep with her. It was like the drier her personality was, the more attracted people would be. She was pretty sure they mistook her for being mysterious when really, she was just boring.

"What's good here?"

The customer had red hair dye, made obvious by the blonde roots. Her khaki trench coat hung loosely around her thin frame, and the heels on her platform boots were at least six inches. She was older than Francis, though not by much. Perhaps four or five years.

"Um, the meatball sub's pretty popular," Francis told her. "But I like the tuna melt."

"Tuna it is."

Francis could feel the woman's eyes on her as she made the sandwich. While they waited for it to toast, the woman asked if she worked there every day.

"Almost every day. I get Mondays off."

She took the sandwich out of the oven and wrapped it up. The woman paid for it and put a five in the tip jar.

"I'll see ya around," she remarked before giving Francis a wink.

Three days later, on a Sunday, the woman returned. Her roots had been touched up. She ordered a chicken salad sandwich and slipped Francis a Post-it.

"Call me tomorrow," she said. "I'll take you to my gallery."

When the woman left, Francis looked at the note. Above the number, she had written *NATASHA*.

The next morning, Francis texted her two words:

tuna melt

The gallery was filled with overly saturated photographs of women printed on canvas. Some of the subjects were nude. Some wore ball gowns. Others were covered in glitter from head to toe.

At the front desk, a goth receptionist painted her nails.

Natasha led Francis through each section, pointing out which shots she thought were "immortal" and "radical."

"We host about six photographers at a time, then change the selection every few months."

Francis kept her arms crossed for fear of accidentally brushing against something. She didn't know what to say, so she gave Natasha short responses. Natasha didn't appear put off by it. She rambled happily until they finished the tour.

"Wow, uh . . . thanks for showing me all that," Francis said. Did she sound uninterested? "It was neat," she added.

Natasha laughed. "You're kinda strange, huh? Are you hungry?"

They grabbed coffee and a bite at a trendy brunch spot nearby. The place was packed for a Monday, but Natasha knew the head chef. She insisted on picking up the tab, and even ordered Francis another vanilla latte to go.

Natasha's apartment wasn't much bigger than hers, but it was newer, cleaner, and had an actual sense of interior design.

Francis sat on the red velvet couch drinking her latte while Natasha poured herself a glass of white wine. They made small talk about books and television shows, the state of the economy. She thought Natasha was too easily amused. Francis knew she wasn't the most fascinating person—nowhere even remotely close—and yet Natasha acted like Francis was some sort of maven.

She found she was fond, however, of how Natasha had this careless air about her. Things sort of magically worked for her, like how when she couldn't find the corkscrew, she casually opened the wine bottle with a knife. Francis found that comforting, so she decided to carry on.

She finished her latte, and they moved to the bedroom. The experience was a bit unsettling. Natasha was too generous, and that made Francis uncomfortable. Plus, the sheets looked expensive. Francis felt like they were spoiling them.

When they were done, Natasha offered a matinee movie showing before dinner.

"I'm sorry," Francis said. "I think I want to go home."

Natasha flipped her hair. "That's fine. My husband will be home soon anyway."

Natasha called her a cab, and they parted with a hug. On the ride home, Francis took out her phone and resaved Natasha's contact name as "Gallery Lady (Married)."

When she returned to her apartment, Francis was surprised to find a familiar light shining across her kitchen floor. She hurried to the oven, where she found exactly what she had hoped for.

As she dug into the second such miraculous gift, she was pleased to discover it was rhubarb. It was more buttery than the other one, and warmer too. She had to keep her mouth open so the portions wouldn't burn her tongue, and despite still being full from brunch, Francis devoured every morsel. She ran her fingers through the pink juice at the bottom of the pan and licked them clean.

For the next two weeks, Francis didn't think about Natasha. She worked her usual shifts at the deli, staying after closing every night to sweep all the lettuce. Mr. Do seemed to get off her back and even let her take longer breaks.

"You just like my daughter," he told her. "So much potential, but nowhere to go."

What Francis couldn't stop thinking about was the pies. What did they mean? Did they only appear after she'd had sex with strangers? Would they be different flavors each time?

One evening, when she'd finished her dinner—a bitten-into BLT rejected by a customer—Francis dialed her best and only friend, Conrad.

Conrad picked up after two rings. "Oh, god, what do you want?"

"Love you too."

"Yeah, yeah."

"Something weird is going on."

There was a pause.

"Tell me more."

Francis took a moment to think about how best to explain. Eventually, she said, "Pies are appearing in my oven after I have sex."

Hmm. That probably wasn't the right wording.

"Fuck, are you on something?"

"No, Conrad, I'm telling you! I've slept with two people in the past three weeks, and each time, a freshly baked pie just . . . appeared in my oven. You have to believe me."

"Okay, I believe you. What do you want me to do about it?"

Francis took a deep breath. "I want you to sleep with me."

There was another pause, then, "You *are* on something. I'm calling Regina."

"Do *not* bring my godmother into this! I'll kill you. Look, I know it's a big ask . . ."

"Big ask?! It's . . . it's EW, Francis. You're like my sister!"

"Conrad, please! Listen. There's something about these pies. They're . . . the *best* pies I've ever had *in my life*. Plus, I have no idea how this whole thing works, and I want to find out more. Just think of it as a . . . a science experiment."

"Couldn't you just pick someone up at a bar? Why do *I* have to do this?"

"Because. I wanna see if it's different with someone I know."

There was silence. Then a sigh. Then a groan.

When he arrived at her apartment, Conrad immediately pushed by her as he tore the beanie off his head. He went to the kitchen, opened the oven, and stared. Then he closed it and glanced at the garbage can. The empty aluminum pans were peeking out beneath days' worth of takeout boxes.

"You finished both of them?"

Francis nodded.

"Shit. You're not joking, are you?"

She shook her head.

Conrad threw his beanie onto the ground and ran both hands through his hair. Then he kicked off his slip-on Vans and ripped off his denim jacket before pacing back and forth.

"Come on, Conrad. You don't want to be a virgin forever, do you?"

"Fuck you."

"Please do."

"You are *so* annoying."

"Okay, how 'bout this? If you do this for me, I'll get Regina to buy us tickets to Deathstar Dragons."

"Fuck you."

"You keep saying that, but you—"

"Okay, I'll do it! Shut up already!" He grabbed a tuft of his hair and let it go with a groan. "How are we doing this?"

"Well, I was thinking we do it on the couch. That way, we can keep an eye on the oven."

"I didn't mean *where,* you psycho, I meant *HOW.*"

They both looked at the couch. Francis moved over to it, shoved the pile of unfolded laundry onto the floor, and began unbuttoning her shirt.

"Stop, stop, stop!" Conrad yelled. "Ugh! Just . . . take off your pants."

He faced the stove as Francis slipped off her jeans. Then he started walking backward toward the couch.

"You're good, keep going," Francis guided him. "Don't trip over the rug. Keep going. Okay, stop."

"Are you lying down?" he asked.

"Yeah."

Conrad unbuckled his belt and let his pants fall. "Don't look at my ass."

"I'm not."

"Close your eyes."

"I am."

After what felt like forever, Francis felt his body fuse with hers. His skin was cool and hairless. She opened her eyes.

"I hate you so much," he said.

She turned her head to face the oven. They had the perfect view.

"Okay," she told him. "Do it."

He fumbled for a bit.

"Lower," Francis said.

"Can you shut up so I can think about something else?"

Conrad was awkward, as she'd expected, but he eventually stopped talking once he found a rhythm. Francis kept her gaze on the oven the entire time, willing the light to turn on. At one point, she feared she had done it wrong. Perhaps it wouldn't happen if she had eyes on it.

Then, just as she sensed Conrad getting tired, there was a click followed by the illumination of her dreams.

"No fucking way." Conrad pulled himself off her and slipped back into his briefs.

Francis hurriedly sifted her panties out of her crumpled jeans, nearly tripped putting them on, and ran to the oven.

She poked the pie with her finger. It was only slightly warm, so she removed it with her bare hands and put it on the counter.

Francis looked around. She hadn't done the dishes, and there weren't any clean forks left, so she grabbed a spoon.

"You want some?" she asked.

"Fuck no. That thing *literally* just popped up. What if it's cursed? I'm not eating some woo-woo witch cake."

"Pie."

"Whatever!"

Francis dug into her prize. The fruit pieces were somehow both soft and crunchy, sweet and tart. The crust was an impeccable golden brown. The filling was sprinkled with thinly sliced almonds.

"It's pear."

Conrad appeared beside her. "What?! That's bullshit!"

"What's wrong with pear?"

"It's basic."

"No, it's not. Apple's basic."

"It's not me."

"Yes, it is. It's . . . casually artsy. Like one of those still life Renaissance paintings at an Italian restaurant."

"I'm not watching you eat that."

Face scrunched, Conrad put on the rest of his clothes and power walked to the door.

"Don't talk to me for a month," he told her just before the door slammed.

Francis carried the pie to the living room and turned on the television. She watched reruns of game shows until the streets grew quiet. Another empty tin graced the trash can.

During the week, she texted her godmother about the Deathstar Dragons concert. Then she called Conrad.

"Hey."

"I told you not to talk to me."

"Let's do it again."

"Oh, I see what's going on—you're *actually* insane."

"Don't you wanna know if it'll work twice? Or whether it'd be pear again? Aren't you the least bit curious?"

"Not at all."

"All right, fine. I'm sorry. Anyway, I got the tickets."

"Really?"

"Yeah. For the eleventh."

"Fuck yes."

Francis hung up. Her cravings were getting stronger, and she knew she'd have to do something about it soon. So, after her shift that night, she headed to the western-themed bar down the street.

There were only two men at the bar. One was in his fifties, practically wearing a costume with his cowboy hat and stiff flannel. Francis was pretty sure he was bald under the hat.

The other was blacked out, drooling on the bar counter as he slept.

The bartender wore a wedding band.

Francis sighed and sat beside Cowboy Hat. *Who knows? Maybe an older man will be a better lover than Cable Guy.*

The door swung open. Francis turned. She recognized him immediately.

"Kaleb."

"Yooooo, Fran Fran. It's been a minute!"

Kaleb wrapped his long arms around her. Cowboy Hat downed his beer in disappointment, slapped a dollar beside the glass, and left the bar.

"Damn, how long has it been?" Kaleb wondered, taking the stool beside her.

"I don't know, six years?"

"Holy shit."

Francis noticed he'd gained a pound or ten since high school, yet he still had the same charm. His hair was shorter now. He had a beard growing in, and he'd gotten an earring since she last saw him.

The bartender approached them. As Kaleb ordered rum and Coke for two, Francis texted Conrad.

> *at bar with Kaleb from hs*
> *Kaleb Kissinger? oh god, don't do it*
> *y not? he's nice*
> *u need help*

"Do you live here?" Kaleb asked.

Francis stuffed her phone into her pocket and nodded.

"Good for you, Fran. It's nice when people actually leave their hometowns, you know? What do you do out here?"

"I, uh—I do PR for this start-up," she lied. "It's nothing. What about you? Do you live here?"

"Just moved here, actually. I got a job in Midtown. Advertising."

"Nice. So, are you . . . meeting someone here?"

"Oh," Kaleb chuckled. "You wouldn't believe it. I was supposed to meet a date at the restaurant across the street. Got stood up."

"Damn."

"Right? I figured, I'm already out. Might as well get a drink. And from the looks of it, I made the right move."

Francis smiled.

Not long after, they were walking through the city, passing closed boutiques and open pizza parlors, technically closed but practically open parks.

Kaleb talked about his job, though a lot of it went over her head. She studied his face as he rambled, trying to decide whether she found him attractive. He wasn't handsome enough for her to be annoyed, but he didn't have the type of face that one could get sick of either. No, he had the sort of face she could see herself looking at for a very long time.

Then again, Francis knew better than to trust her own judgment. There were many past lovers she had thought the same about. None of them lasted for more than a month. They would all eventually repulse her, either by the way they chewed their food or simply by them being there far too much.

But after Kaleb casually removed a pigeon feather that had landed in her hair, Francis found herself leading him to her apartment. There, he sat on her couch munching on week-old tortilla chips from a plastic bowl while she did the dishes.

"I'm sorry about the mess," she said as he watched her. "And I know this is a terrible time to do dishes."

"No worries," he replied. "I'm chillin'."

"And I'm sorry I don't have any salsa."

"Like I said, I'm chillin'."

Kaleb stood, taking the bowl with him to the mantel. He examined the eclectic four-by-six picture frames she'd gotten from the thrift store.

"These your folks?"

Francis scrubbed a fork. "Uh, yeah. They actually died when I was eleven."

Kaleb dropped a piece of chip on the carpet. "What? I didn't know that. That's crazy."

"It's no biggie."

"How did I not know that?"

"I don't know."

Kaleb set the bowl on the coffee table and walked over to the sink. He turned off the faucet, ripped off the last paper towel from the roll on the counter, and held it out to her.

"Come on," he said. "That's enough dishes. Let's hang out."

Francis dried her hands and plopped down onto the couch next to him.

"Want some chips?" he asked.

"I'm good."

Kaleb turned to her and held both her hands. "That sucks about your parents, Fran Fran. How are you doing these days?"

Francis looked at him. "I work at a deli," she confessed. "I don't do PR. I make sandwiches."

He let go of her hands. She thought he would be weirded out or upset, leave her apartment, maybe. But instead, he grabbed the chip bowl and continued munching.

"It was actually my ex who stood me up," he told her. "Honestly, I moved out here thinking we could give it another go, but I was obviously delusional."

"Damn."

"Damn is right."

He set the bowl down again. "Those chips are kinda stale."

"I know."

Kaleb leaned his back against the armrest, putting his feet up so he could look at her. "I'm proud of you, Fran Fran. Look at you—you're out here alone, working your ass off. Most people don't do that."

"Oh . . . it's nothing like that."

"It is, though. You're cool. I mean, you were cool back then, but you're *really* cool now."

Francis's eyes flickered toward the pile of clothes on the floor. She could feel Kaleb trying his best to ignore it.

She leaned onto the other armrest. They were now facing each other, their legs practically intertwined.

"Why did we stop hanging out?" she asked him. "What happened junior year?"

"Man, that year was stupid. It was all cliques and shit. I think I just got busy with track and field. Plus, you were always hanging out with that one guy . . . what was his name?"

"Conrad."

"That's right. Funky dude."

"He moved out here, too. We're still friends."

"Oh. Anyway, you were hard to approach. You had this thing about you . . . I dunno what it is. I was intimidated, I think."

He sat up and placed his hands on her knees. "We should have hung out, though. I was stupid."

Kaleb's green eyes bore into hers. Francis hoped she wasn't blushing.

"You're here now," she said softly. Her own tone surprised her.

"I am."

They started to make out, and for a moment, Francis almost forgot about the oven. But as Kaleb fiddled with the hooks of her bra, she felt an exhaustion that morphed into numbness, then melted into sadness.

"I'm sorry," she said. "I know this is a dick move, but I don't think I wanna do this."

Kaleb let out a sigh as he leaned away from her.

"It's not you," she assured him. "This happens with everyone."

"What happens?"

"I don't know. Like, I think I want it, but then I don't."

"That's a waste."

Francis whipped her head toward him. "What did you say?"

"I just mean, you're hot, you know? It's a waste."

She got up from the couch. "Please leave."

"What?"

"I'd like you to leave."

"What'd I do?"

"Get out!"

"Jesus Christ, all right! I'm leaving."

He grabbed the last chip out of the bowl before making his way to the door.

"I always knew you were a crazy bitch."

She could hear him muttering to himself the entire way down the hall, and when the noise faded, Francis threw herself back onto the couch and sobbed. She screamed into one of three mismatched pillows before throwing it across the room. Then she stared at the darkness behind her oven window.

What was wrong with her? Why'd she have to go and screw that up? All she'd had to do was get it over with. How would she satisfy her craving now? She realized she hadn't eaten anything since her afternoon break. It was almost midnight, and all the markets were closed.

Francis stood, fumbled for her keys inside her jacket, and went downstairs to the nearest bodega.

The clerk eyed her as she browsed the shelves. She grabbed flour, sugar, graham crackers, plain potato chips, and a jar of Nutella. From the fridge, she got milk and butter.

"Do you have any cream?" she called out. The clerk shook his head.

Francis grabbed a handful of mini half-and-half cups by the coffee machine, then took a cluster of bananas from the rotating rack by the register. She let everything in her arms tumble onto the counter and dug in her pocket for cash. The clerk dropped the items into a plastic bag and handed it to her.

Back at her apartment, Francis grabbed the chip bowl from the coffee table and dumped the crumbs into the sink. She poured flour into the bowl and threw in a stick of butter. She added water, a bit of sugar, and crumbled graham crackers. She rolled out the dough with an empty bottle of tonic water from her recycling bin, then fished an aluminum pan out of the trash and rinsed it out.

After carefully pressing the dough all around the pan, she made a custard with sliced bananas, Nutella, eggs, milk, and half-and-half. She poured the mixture into the pan, beat up a bag of potato chips—again with the tonic water bottle—and sprinkled the remnants on top. Lastly, she placed the pan in the oven.

Fifteen minutes later, Francis grabbed a clean fork. Steam rose from her masterwork. She probably should have let it cool, but she was famished.

The potato chips made a soft but satisfying *crunch* as she stabbed into the filling. She blew on the hot glob before popping it into her mouth.

With each swallow, her stomach was filled with extraordinary warmth and satisfaction. She savored every dollop of hazelnutty chocolate, every scoop of molten ripe banana, every grain of potato-chip salt, and every flake of perfectly burnt graham cracker crust.

When she had consumed it all, she tore off her clothes and crawled into bed, where she slept deeply and soundlessly.

The next morning, she baked herself another.

The Fifth Will Plead

She was used to the blazing fire, but she never thought it would devour her own home. The smell of gasoline wafted into the depths of her nose as she crawled across the carpet of her bedroom to the door. She knew it was too late, but she felt the knob anyway. It stung her fingers before she could pull away. The flames were beginning to seep through the bottom crack of the door, flickering in and out like a cat clawing beneath it.

She would have to go out the window. The jump might break her leg, but it wasn't anything she hadn't gone through before.

She ran over and tried to slide the window upward. It refused to budge.

Frantically searching the room, she yanked the dial phone from her bedside table and pounded its body against the glass. It wasn't going to work.

She should have known better, but desperation overtook her wit.

Besides, why wouldn't the window open? It wasn't a faulty one—she opened it constantly.

The smell of gas hit her again, and suddenly, she knew. The realization traveled through her entire being, attacking her chest, her gut. Yes, she was almost sure of it. The window. The gas. The fact that she hadn't cooked anything for months.

Someone wanted her dead.

Sirens blared through the neighborhood until they were close enough to deafen. She could see her team through the hole in the window, rushing out of the truck she had driven many times. Chief shouted something, but it was lost in the inferno that engulfed her.

She tried the window again to no avail.

They need to stand back, she determined. *They need to—*

She heard it first. A boom—then the crack of bone as she was flung against the wall.

Detective Kani Victur swallowed a shot of bile that had risen from her throat. She was used to grisly scenes, but the remnants of this one were different.

"Name's Elaine Maverick," Detective Tom Pertran told her. His eyes avoided the corpse's charred fingers and draping tissue. "She was a firefighter at Station 33. Ironic."

Kani glanced at the crew weaving around the black skeleton of a house. "Source?"

"Gasoline. The stove's being examined as we speak. Her team managed to pull her out, but she was dead before she touched the lawn. They were going to bring the body to the hospital, but the fire chief had enough sense to think this a crime scene."

Kani reached into the pocket of her bomber jacket for a notepad.

"What made him think that?"

"Elaine couldn't open her window. Like it was glued shut or something. He thought it was strange."

"Hm."

"How was the night out with your sister?" Tom asked.

"Same as always," Kani replied. "She and Lawrence bickered until she got drunk enough for them to make out."

Tom pulled out a pack of cigs, remembered where they were, and put it away. "You ever think about marrying someone?"

Kani scoffed. "Were there any other victims?"

Tom shook his head. "She lived alone. A few of the responders had minor injuries from the explosion."

A fly landed on Kani's writing hand. She was about to swat it away when she noticed it was on its back, spinning in circles between her knuckles. After staring at it for a moment, she flicked it off and scratched at the spot.

"Tess wants you over for dinner," Tom told her. "Says she misses 'Con-Con.' Anyway, Holly's making some sort of pineapple roast tonight."

Kani smiled. "I miss little Tessie, too. And Holly's cooking. I just, uh—have been needed at home lately."

Tom gave a nod of understanding as a fire inspector approached them.

"Detectives," the inspector said. "Bad news, I'm afraid."

Tom straightened his fedora. "What is it?"

"The source is gasoline, all right. But it was found everywhere. The kitchen, the living room, the hall . . . the chief was right. This was arson. Someone was inside before it happened."

"Kani? That you?"

Kani hung her keys on the hook by the fridge and grabbed a cold beer. "Who else would it be, Mom?"

She walked from the kitchen into the living room where her mother sat on the faded leather recliner she'd been in for two decades. *The Carol Burnett Show* was softly playing on the television, igniting the darkness in multicolored flashes.

"You can't be too safe," her mother said without looking at her. "You of all people should know that."

Kani plopped onto the couch beside her and cracked open the can. "No one's going to get you, Mom. I promise. Did you finish the plate I fixed you?"

"Some. The chicken was a bit dry."

"Didn't I tell you to put gravy on it?"

"I forgot."

Kani kicked off her shoes on the blotchy carpet, pulled her gun out of the holster, and placed it on the coffee table.

"I saw that fire on the news," her mother told her. "You got any idea who did it?"

Kani took a sip from the can. "Talked to some neighbors today, but no one saw anything. Her parents doubt she had any enemies. We're stuck right now."

"Mm. You got back real late last night," her mother said. "Keyla get drunk again?"

"Yeah, but it wasn't too bad."

"I don't know what she expected, marrying a mechanic."

Kani shrugged. "They're in love. I think they'll be fine."

"As long as they don't have children."

"She wanted to see you," said Kani. "I told her you'd be asleep."

"Mm."

A political ad came on the screen. "*Mayor Akida cares more about the dead than the living*," the voiceover bellowed. "*She wants to stop the build on the Doe Creek lot because it's 'sacred land.' But what about the increase of homelessness in the city?*"

"People will attack her for anything," Kani's mother remarked. "That's what happens when you got a lady mayor. It's like what you deal with as the only lady in your precinct."

In the kitchen, the fridge began its daily hum.

"I should probably eat something," Kani sighed.

"Help me up," her mother said. "I gotta use the toilet."

Kani put the beer can on the table, stained with a dozen water rings. Her mother clutched the cane leaning on the side of the recliner as Kani hooked her arm and lifted all three hundred pounds.

"You want me to walk you?"

"No, no. I got it. You make yourself a plate."

As her mother shuffled down the hall, she called out, "Oh, and take out the trash. There have been flies. Weird little things, too, spinning around."

The first ring woke her at 5:33 a.m.

On the second ring, Kani rolled over to her nightstand and took the phone off the receiver.

"Sorry, Victur," Tom said. "Hope I didn't wake your ma. We got another one."

"Another fire?"

"No. You're gonna want to meet us at the beach."

Before long, Kani found herself freezing against the wind, staring at the body of a woman face down in the sand.

"A local was going on his morning jog," Tom said, blowing into his gloves. "Spotted the body on the shore. Thought it was some sort of shark at first."

Kani looked at him. "Morning jog? At this hour? That's some dedication."

"I know what you're thinking," Tom answered, "but his story checks out. Wife confirmed he does it every day, and a few neighbors can too."

Kani tried to hold her pen steady in the cold as she jotted that down.

"Here." Tom started to tear off his gloves, but Kani swatted her hand to stop him.

"I'm fine."

Some yards away, a crime scene investigator shouted at a nosy woman walking her dog to step away from the scene.

"How long have you all been here?" Kani asked Tom. "I'm sick of Gil not calling me."

"Don't mind him," Tom told her. "You know he's a dillwad. I secretly call him Gillwad."

Kani didn't laugh. She slipped her hands into her pockets and got closer to the body.

Defeated, Tom followed her. "They're working on identification," he said. "She didn't have anything on her."

"Do we know how long she's been dead?"

"A couple hours. The incident would have happened between two and four a.m."

Kani crouched as low as she could, trying to get a glimpse of the victim's face. Though she could only see the cheeks, she could tell the woman was in her late twenties or early thirties, the same as Elaine.

"What do you think? Same guy?" she asked.

Tom shook his head. "I don't know. The timing's convenient, but the MO doesn't match. Maybe she got drunk, passed out, and the high tide drowned her."

A wave glided toward them and stopped an inch from the victim's head. That's when Kani noticed the few flies spinning on their backs atop the wet sand.

"I wish it wasn't too windy for a smoke," Tom muttered.

Kani stood and looked around. There were a few houses lining the shore, but most had windows obscured by trees. They were also about a hundred yards away, so any noise would have been muffled by the waves. It was unlikely anyone would have witnessed what happened, especially in the dark.

In other words, if anyone wanted to kill someone on the beach, this would have been the perfect spot to do it.

"Pertran!" a voice called.

Kani sighed. Tom gave her an empathetic shrug as he walked over to Sergeant Gil. When he returned, she knew by the look on his face that they had their work cut out for them.

"What is it?" she asked.

He held his fedora down as a gust of wind blew at them both. "Cause of death was drowning."

Kani nodded. "And based on the marks around her head, I think it's safe to assume it was an attack."

"That's not all. They've identified her. Name's Morgan Frey." Tom's eyes moved from side to side.

"Just say it," Kani pressed over the roar of a wave.

"She was a navy sailor."

At the station, Tom warmed his hands around a cup of coffee as Kani pinned photos and notes up on a bulletin board.

"Look, it could be a coincidence," Tom suggested. "A random arsonist for the first victim, and an argument gone wrong for this one."

Kani stopped to give him a look.

"I heard it when I said it," he said, slurping his coffee. "Just trying to be optimistic."

They were interrupted by Chief Price knocking on the doorframe.

"Look, folks," he said, chewing on a stick of jerky, "you already know this, but we're gonna have a lot of people breathing down our necks. We're spending all our resources on these cases. What do you have so far?"

"There has to be a connection," Kani replied. "We just have to figure out what it is. We'll interview friends and family of our two victims. See if they're connected by anybody in their lives."

"Let's go back to Elaine Maverick's family today," Tom agreed.

Chief Price entered the room and examined the bulletin board. He sighed, finished his jerky, and wiped his hands across his protruding belly.

"Victur," he said. "I know you've only been detective two years, but don't fuck this up. I don't need the sergeants telling me 'I told you so.'"

She gave him a nod. When Chief Price was gone, Tom walked to the board.

"All right, let's start simple," he said. "What do the two victims have in common?"

"They're women. Around the same age."

"Right. What else?"

The two of them stood in silence for a while.

Kani shook her head. "We've got a firefighter and a navy sailor . . ."

Sergeant Gil popped up at the door. "Got anything, Pertran?"

Kani crossed her arms. "You know I'm a detective, too, Sergeant."

"Yeah, so?"

"So you need to talk to me as much as you do Tom. And you need to call us *both* whenever we have a victim."

"I call Tom, he calls you. What's the big deal?"

"The *big deal* is—" Kani's eyes lit up. "That's it!"

Tom watched as she hurried to the board.

"Do we know if Morgan Frey had a family?" she asked.

Sergeant Gil picked at a tooth. "Not married. She lived with her dad."

Tom sat and leaned back in his chair. "You think these were dates gone wrong, Victur?"

"It's possible, but that's not what—"

"Single women are more commonly victims," Sergeant Gil interrupted. "If you're trying to burn someone's house down, or drown them at the beach, it's a hell of a lot easier when they're alone, isn't it? It doesn't mean anything."

Kani forced her lips into a smile.

"Sure. But how many female firefighters and navy sailors do you know, Sergeant?"

Tom stroked his chin, letting out a puff of air. "He hates women in power."

"Women in male-dominated jobs," Kani corrected. "I don't know how much power a firefighter really has."

"So, what?" Sergeant Gil asked.

Kani rolled her eyes. "That helps us find our suspect. We're looking for a guy who wouldn't like the idea of women working these types of jobs. Untraditional women."

Sergeant Gil guffawed. "That's the whole damn world! Great work, *Detective*. You'll find this guy in no time."

He shook his head as he left the room.

"Okay, so a firefighter killed by fire," Tom said. "A navy sailor killed by water. This guy definitely has a sick sense of humor. And the skill it takes to carry it out makes me think white-collar."

Kani pondered for a bit. "I don't know. A man with a white-collar job means he's doing well for himself. What reason would he have to resent these women?"

Tom shrugged. "Maybe they beat him in a round of golf?"

Minutes later, they were standing in the office before the rest of their team.

"We're looking for a male between the ages of thirty-five to fifty," Kani told them. "Blue-collar job. Traditional views. High possibility of being married."

"He probably wouldn't treat his wife like a queen, either," Tom added.

"Detective Pertran and I are going to interview Elaine Maverick's family to see if there was anyone in her life that fits that description," Kani stated. "The rest of you should be scouring records for possible suspects. Look for construction workers, garbage men, anything you can think of."

Sergeant Gil scoffed. "That's all we got to go off of? You got hundreds of guys in the city who'd fit that description."

"Yeah, but not all of them are killers," Kani said. "Cross-check them with criminal records. Use your best instincts. This is all we've got for now."

As the team dispersed, a sergeant approached them.

"Victur, your sister's on line three."

Kani groaned. "Sorry, Tom. Give me a moment?"

"Of course."

At her desk, Kani took a deep breath before putting her ear to the receiver.

"What is it?"

"Can you meet me at The Five Dive today? I need to talk to you about something."

Tom sat on the edge of his desk across from her, listening.

"Is it urgent? I have a job, Keyla."

"I know, I know. Just . . . tell me what time works for you."

Kani looked at the clock. "Fine. Be there at four."

She hung up and looked at Tom. "I gotta meet Keyla after we talk to the Mavericks."

"Let's make a stop first," he replied, grabbing his coat and fedora. "Trust me."

Not long after, they were sitting at a table in a diner. Kani dipped a fry in mustard as she witnessed Tom scarf down an entire burger in four bites.

"I can't believe you have an appetite right now," Kani said.

"I have a feeling this case is going to consume us," Tom told her. "It'll be better if we fill our stomachs before that happens."

A group of women in cropped vests and bell-bottoms headed toward the exit. They made eyes at Tom and giggled as they passed.

"Okay, Casanova," Kani teased.

"Yeah, yeah."

Tom wiped his hands on a napkin and inhaled half his cola through a straw.

"These women's outfits are getting silly," Kani remarked, staring at the group through the window. "Are they not freezing?"

"Lighten up, Victur. It's the seventies—it's all about freedom of expression. At least they don't wear the same bomber every day, even when it's hot out."

"Touché."

"You want another plate of fries?"

"No, thanks. I don't have much time. Let's get to the Mavericks."

"Slow down, will ya?"

Kani raised an eyebrow. "What's this really about, Tom?"

Her partner sighed. "I'm worried this is going to be *that* case for you."

"What do you mean?"

"You know . . . the case that haunts you. We all got one."

"You don't think we're going to solve this?" Kani asked, brow furrowed.

Tom clicked his tongue. "I don't know. I hope we do. But if we don't . . ." He looked at her. "I'm just worried, is all. I don't want you to beat yourself up."

Kani played with the steel sauce container in front of her and gazed at the glob of ketchup inside. "I'm going to solve this one, Tom. But not if we keep sitting at this table."

Tom stood, downed the rest of his cola, and slipped a bill under the cup.

"Oh, here," Kani said, pulling out her wallet. "Let me."

"Would you relax? I got it. Get your butt outside and in the damn car, Victur."

"Fine, but I'm driving."

The Mavericks' house was a cobalt-blue oasis with a trimmed garden surrounded by a white picket fence. No one would know looking at it that grief welled within, threatening to drown its occupants.

"She was our only child," Mr. Maverick told them, weeping behind his horn-rimmed glasses.

Mrs. Maverick sat silently beside him on the couch with her chin down and hands folded in her lap.

Across from them, Kani and Tom adjusted themselves in uncomfortable neon-yellow chairs that the Mavericks had brought in from the dining room.

"I told her not to move out," Mr. Maverick continued. "I didn't want her living alone. She wouldn't listen."

"I'm sorry, sir," Kani said. "We believe her death is connected to another victim's."

"It's that navy sailor, isn't it?" Mr. Maverick asked, taking off his glasses to wipe them on his shirt.

"You think the arsonist also killed that woman?"

"It's likely," Tom confirmed. "We believe the killer is a man who works a blue-collar job. Did Elaine have anyone in her life that fits that description? A boyfriend, perhaps?"

Mr. Maverick shook his head. "Absolutely not. Not to be rude, but we're well-off, as you can see. We wouldn't allow her to date . . . someone like that."

"How about just a friend?" Kani asked. "Anyone at all."

"Not that I know of," Mr. Maverick replied. "Most of her time was spent at the station. Anyone she knew would be there. You know, the family business would have gone to her. But Elaine . . . she wanted to fight fires. I could never understand why."

"We've taken enough of your time," Tom said. "Thank you, Mr. and Mrs. Maverick. Again, we're sorry for your loss."

They all stood.

"Please call us if you think of anything," Kani told them as Mrs. Maverick led them to the door. From outside, she could hear Mr. Maverick blowing his nose in the kitchen.

The chill hit them as she and Tom stepped toward the car.

"Detectives!" Mrs. Maverick called after them.

Kani turned. "Yes?"

"I just remembered something."

They got closer to her. "Sure. What is it?" Kani asked.

Mrs. Maverick held onto the doorknob as she spoke. "A few weeks ago, Elaine had a plumber come to the house. Now, it could be nothing, but . . ."

"No, that's good," Kani assured her. "Do you know who the plumber is?"

"Unfortunately not. Any information she would've kept was lost in the fire."

"Okay. We'll look into it. Thank you."

When the door shut, Tom took out a cigarette.

"Well, a plumber certainly fits our description," he said.

Kani nodded. "Will you drop me off at The Five? I gotta meet Keyla. In the meantime, go to Morgan Frey's home and talk to her father. Check the house for plumbing receipts."

"Roger that."

The last time Kani found herself at the dive bar was three months ago, after she had nearly been killed responding to a bank robbery. The guy who'd shot at her had suffered a mental breakdown from losing all his cash at a two-star casino hotel. He'd gotten her left arm, barely missing her heart. She'd then insisted Tom take her for a drink to numb the pain. She wanted to visit the bar before the hospital, but of course, Tom had refused. So, they'd hit the bar after she was discharged.

Keyla was already sitting at a booth when Kani entered. The lights were much too dim for it being four o'clock, and the young bartender seemed unenthused that he had another customer to attend to.

"I got us beer," her sister said as Kani sat across from her.

"Thanks." Kani took a sip of foam. "What the hell are you wearing?"

Keyla looked down. "What? It's a shirt."

"Why are there holes in it?"

"It's knitted, Kani. God, you have no sense of fashion."

"I can practically see your nipples."

"Look, I know you're busy," Keyla said, "so

I'll cut to the case. Lawrence and I are moving in with his folks. Tomorrow."

Kani choked. "What? They're three hundred miles away."

"I know. I meant to tell you at dinner the other day, but I chickened out."

"Keyla, what's going on? What's the rush?"

"I'm pregnant."

". . . Oh."

They sat in silence for a moment.

"They'd help out with the baby," Keyla continued. "We wouldn't have to worry about rent. It'll be good for us. Anyway, our lease ends today, and we don't want to pay for another month."

"Yeah, yeah. I got it."

Kani took a gulp of her beer, avoiding eye contact.

"Please don't be upset," Keyla pleaded.

"Who said I'm upset?"

"I can tell, Kani. You're my sister."

Kani tapped her fingers on the side of the glass. "This is just really sudden."

Keyla gave a small smile. "I know. But I'm excited, really. I don't want you to feel like you did when—" She stopped herself.

"When what?"

Keyla shifted in her seat, regretting her words. Finally, she said, "When Dad left."

"We can have this conversation without mentioning Dad."

"Sorry . . . I was just worried. I mean, I was too young, but he could have left you with an explanation. A postcard. Anything."

"He left me with a truck," Kani joked. "It's beat-up now, but it gets me around. Besides, it's not me you need to worry about. Have you even *thought* about Mom? What if something were to happen to me? Who would take care of her?"

"Nothing's going to happen to you, Kani. And if something did, I'd obviously figure it out."

"'Figure it out'? As in putting her in a nursing home?"

"I didn't say that."

Kani leaned back in her seat and let out a sigh. "Okay. I'm sorry. I'm happy for you. I am."

"Thank you."

Keyla signaled to the bartender to fill her glass.

"Haven't you heard about that new study?" Kani asked her. "Alcohol's bad for pregnant women."

"It's all bullshit," Keyla replied. She thanked the bartender as he brought them a pitcher.

Kani shrugged. "Fine, don't listen to the experts." She took a sip and wiped her lips with the back of her hand. "Hey, sis."

"What?"

"You know a lot about people in this city. Who's a plumber who would have a motive to kill?"

"Are you gonna pay me to do your job for you?"

"Come on."

Keyla sighed. "Let's see . . ." She looked around the motionless bar, as though one of the drunks nodding off might give them the answer.

"Maybe Lawrence would have an idea?" Kani suggested.

Keyla cocked her head in annoyance. "Why would he know?"

"I just thought—"

"Why would you say that? Do all mechanics know plumbers or something? All poor men must know each other, right?"

"You're impossible. Forget I said anything."

At that moment, the bartender shouted from the wall phone, "Lady cop! You got a call."

Kani slid out of the booth. "I'll be right back," she told Keyla. "Stop drinking."

It was Tom on the line. "I'm at Morgan's apartment and, well, I definitely found something."

"Please let it be a receipt."

"Exactamundo. For . . . drumroll . . . Westside Service & Plumbing. Dated eleven weeks before Morgan's death."

"Oh my god. What did her father say?"

"He was here when the guy was here. Knows exactly what he looks like."

"Okay. Come pick me up. We'll get the bastard's address from the company."

Kani hung up and hurried back to Keyla. "I gotta leave soon," she said, sliding into the booth. "We got a lead. A plumber from some company called Westside Service."

"Westside?" Keyla pondered. "That sounds familiar. I think our landlord sent them when we had a leak."

"Really?"

"Yeah. The guy was real nice, though. Showed me pictures of his kids. I'd be surprised if he was a murderer."

"Well, they probably have a few different guys they send out."

"Right."

Kani finished another glass while Keyla pretended to watch *Somerset* on the muted television.

Eventually, a honk outside informed them of Tom's arrival and they both got up from the booth. Kani held back tears as her sister wrapped her arms around her.

"Promise you'll come visit," Keyla said as they hugged. "I want my baby to know her aunt."

"I promise."

According to the manager at Westside, Hal Darnell had been one of their plumbers for over thirty years. He lived with his wife and two sons. The drive to his home wasn't exactly what Kani would call "the slums," but it sure wasn't in the nice parts of the city. She spotted a few stray dogs wandering the neighborhoods and shirtless toddlers playing on rusty front-yard swing sets, though she'd seen much worse on previous cases.

Beside her, Tom was whistling along with the radio as he drove.

"What'd the manager of Westside say again?" Kani asked him. "Darnell was at Maverick's home three weeks before she died, and Frey's apartment when?"

"Eleven weeks before she died."

"Hm." Kani jotted the timing down in her notepad. "What do you think? This our guy? I mean, he's met both victims. But if it's him, he sure took his time before killing them."

"Yeah, but he's the only plumber out of twelve at that company who has a connection to both our victims. That's too strange, in my opinion."

Tom turned off the radio and pulled over. "This is it."

Kani examined the house through the window. It was surprisingly . . . normal. Toys were scattered on the kept lawn, a water-filled birdbath stood beneath a tree, and the curtains were wide open. If this was their guy, he'd done a damn good job at hiding it.

They got out of the car and approached the front door. Before knocking, Tom gave Kani a look as if to say, "Ready?"

A boy about five years old greeted them. He was wearing pajamas and had a small scar on his forehead.

"Hi there," Tom chirped. "Are your parents home?"

The boy nodded, glancing at the gun on Kani's hip.

"Who is it, son?" a man's voice called from inside.

"It's the police!" the boy yelled.

A man about fifty showed himself at the door. He was balding, wore suspenders across a stained white T-shirt, and had black dirt marks all over his hands. Kani tried to get a read on him as she looked into his crystal-blue eyes.

"Are you Hal Darnell?" Tom asked.

The man looked down at his son. "Go to your room and play with your brother. Shut the door. We'll holler when dinner's ready."

When the boy was gone, the man gave Tom a nod. "I'm Hal Darnell. Is something the matter?"

"We're conducting a homicide investigation on victims whose homes you serviced," Kani told him. "Do you mind if we come in to ask you some questions?"

"Homicide?" Hal said. "Heavens. That's awful. I'd be happy to help any way that I can." He opened the door wider to let them in.

"Please excuse my appearance," Hal mentioned. "I got home not too long ago. I like watching the tube for a bit before my shower."

Kani examined the living room. It was tidy, thoughtfully decorated with floral wallpaper, throw pillows, and framed photos of the family scattered about.

Hal gestured to a closed wooden sliding door. "Back there's the kitchen. My wife's making dinner. Better not disturb her."

He gave Kani a smile. She wasn't sure what to make of it.

"Have a seat," Hal told them, lowering himself onto the recliner while they took the couch. "How can I help ya?"

Kani took out her notepad. "Do you remember providing service for a woman named Elaine Maverick about a month ago?"

Hal put his hands on his knees and let out a breath. "I hate to tell ya, but I'm not good with names. Maybe you could describe her?"

"She was a firefighter," Kani elaborated. "She lived in a small two-story home near the station."

"Actually, yes. I do remember her. Hang on, you said 'homicide'—does that mean she's been . . . ?"

Kani squinted. "Do you watch the news much, Mr. Darnell?"

Hal shook his head. "I don't. It's all too sad for me. I like watching sitcoms, game shows, that sort of thing."

Tom and Kani looked at each other. Tom turned back to Hal. "Elaine Maverick's house was burned down," he told him. "She was inside and didn't make it."

Hal sat back in the recliner. His head dropped. "Oh no . . . that's terrible. She was such a nice woman." He looked back up at them. "W-what do you need from me?"

"Did you notice anything out of the ordinary while you were there?" Kani questioned. "Anything out of place? Or something that would cause a gas leak?"

"No, not at all. I mean, there could have been something, but if there was, I sure didn't see it."

Kani studied his mannerisms. He had moved his hands a lot when he spoke before, but now he was still.

"That's all right," she said. "What about a woman named Morgan Frey? She lived with her father in an apartment by the beach. She was in the navy."

Hal's eyes wandered again. "Did her father use a wheelchair? I think so. That was before the firefighter. But I didn't know that she was in the navy—she had normal clothes on. I didn't ask what she did."

"Anything strange about the apartment?" Kani asked.

"Not that one either, no. Wait—did something happen to her, too?"

Kani paused. Hal seemed gentle, charming even. For a balding older man, he wasn't unattractive, either. It was hard to picture him committing those crimes.

"Thank you for giving us your time, Mr. Darnell," she said, giving Tom a nod to let him know she was done.

They stood and Hal followed suit. Just as they were about to head to the door, Kani heard a clang in the kitchen.

She turned. "Do you mind if I ask your wife some questions as well?"

Hal shifted his weight. "Oh, she doesn't like to be disturbed when she's cooking."

"It'll only be a moment," Kani assured, beckoning Tom to follow her as Hal sat back down on his recliner.

When they opened the door, Hal's wife jumped, dropping a spoon on the floor.

"I'm sorry," Kani told her. "We didn't mean to startle you. I'm Detective Kani Victur. This is Detective Tom Pertran."

"Tonya."

Tonya Darnell looked like she'd stepped right out of a 1950s catalog. She wore a yellow long-sleeve dress with a frilly white apron over it. A pearl necklace adorned her neck while red high heels elevated her posture. Stranger still, she was so frail, she could have pulled off being a teenager if it weren't for the lines on her face.

But what startled Kani was the way she looked at Tom. Tonya's eyes widened when she saw him, nearly pressing her back to the counter as she stepped back.

"We were just here to ask your husband some questions about his clients," Kani told her. "Do you mind if we ask you some questions as well?"

Tonya continued staring at Tom, not saying a word.

Kani glanced at her partner. "Maybe I should take this alone," she whispered.

Tom didn't argue. He simply tipped his hat and went back to the living room. When Kani closed the sliding door behind him, Tonya's shoulders lowered. Kani watched as she picked the spoon off the floor and placed it gently in the sink.

"Do you know Detective Pertran?" Kani asked her.

Tonya shook her head.

"Are you sure?"

The woman didn't answer.

Kani took a deep breath. "It's okay," she said. "You can talk to me. What are you making?" She pointed her chin at the boiling pot behind Tonya.

"Stew," Tonya said softly.

"I wish I could cook," Kani remarked. "I'm terrible at it. My mother says so all the time."

She noticed the corner of Tonya's mouth curl upward.

"Do you stay inside all day?" Kani asked.

Tonya nodded. Then, after a moment, she said, "Sometimes I garden."

"I noticed your garden. It's beautiful."

"Thank you."

"I need to ask you something," Kani said sternly. "We're investigating the murders of two women that your husband provided services for. Would you happen to know anything about them?"

Tonya shook her head and lowered the dial on the stove.

"Has your husband ever left in the middle of the night? Maybe you wake up and don't see him in bed?"

"I don't know," Tonya said, thinking. "I take something to help me sleep. It knocks me out."

"You take sleep medication?"

"I was suffering from insomnia, so Hal suggested I get something prescribed."

"Hal suggested that?"

"Yes. Why?"

"Hm."

Kani jotted something down in her notepad.

"P-please," Tonya stammered. "I need to finish preparing dinner. Hal will take his shower soon, and when he's hungry, he gets . . ."

Her voice faded before she smoothed out her apron. "The children get rowdy, is all. I better fill their stomachs so they can settle down."

Tonya rolled up a sleeve and grabbed a ladle, then began stirring the pot on the stove. That was when Kani noticed the bruises on her arm. Tonya let out a small gasp and rolled down her sleeve. She continued stirring.

"Tonya," Kani said delicately. "How did you get those bruises?"

"The boys can be so rough," Tonya chuckled. "I was trying to give them a bath and they fought me."

"Tonya," Kani repeated. "Does Hal hurt you?"

Kani watched as Tonya kept her eyes fixed on the pot, stirring in silence. After a moment, she looked up. "Of course not. He's a decent, God-loving man. He's good to me."

Kani pulled out her card and handed it to her. "Listen. If you ever need help, *anything* at all, you call me. Okay?"

Tonya slipped the card into her apron pocket. Kani opened the door.

"Boys need their fathers," Tonya called after her. "It's important."

"What'd you learn?" Tom asked when they were back in the car.

Kani stared at him. "Why did she look at you like that?"

"Like what?"

"Like she was . . . afraid of you."

"I don't know. Maybe she thought I was someone else. Or she has a bad history with cops."

"It was like she recognized you."

"I don't know what you're talking about, Victur. I just met those people. Same as you."

Kani realized how accusatory she sounded. "You're right. I'm sorry. I'm just so tired."

A voice came over their car radio. "Pertran. Victur. What's your twenty? I repeat. Ten-twenty."

Tom grabbed the speaker. "East side. Over."

"Jesus, you two, where ya been? We've been calling."

"Sorry, Chief," Tom said. "We were entertaining a lead. What's going on?"

"We got another one. You need to come to the airport."

"Yes, Chief. You're sending us out on a flight?"

"Not exactly."

Officers surrounded the entrance of the airport bathroom. The facility was at the corner of the last gate and a closed newsstand. Airport staff told detectives it was a bit of a secret among pilots and stewardesses, helping them avoid lines and crowds.

Kani and Tom slipped under the caution tape and went inside. Sergeant Gil and two other officers were standing in front of a stall.

The body of a woman in a pilot uniform was sprawled across the tiled floor, one arm on the toilet seat. A plastic bag was over her head.

"You thinking what I'm thinking?" Kani asked Tom.

"It's only just occurring to me now," Tom replied. "A pilot. Cause of death—"

"Asphyxiation."

They looked at each other.

"Air," they said simultaneously.

Kani tilted her head. "Or rather, the lack of it."

She studied Tom as he bent down to examine the body. Had he figured that out too easily? She'd been able to, so it was plausible that he had too, right?

"The bathroom certainly fits our plumber theory," Tom noted as he stood.

"An afternoon killing is different," Kani added. "That's risky."

"He's getting bold."

"How'd no one see this guy?"

"Well, there's a 'Closed for Maintenance' floor sign at the entrance. Looks like he placed it there so no one would enter. He could have watched his victim go inside, placed the sign, and followed her in?"

Kani couldn't help but notice how rapidly Tom had come to that conclusion.

"We just saw Hal," Kani said. "He would've had to have done this right before getting home."

"Well, he did say he had just gotten home when we saw him. It's not impossible."

Did he want her to think Darnell was the killer?

Kani turned to Sergeant Gil. "Have the team interview airport staff. We need to find out if a plumber was hired to be here during the time of death. More specifically, a man named Hal Darnell."

To Kani's surprise, Sergeant Gil didn't argue. But he did, of course, provide a groan before walking off with the other two.

When they were gone, Kani pointed at the body.

"Look at the flies," she told Tom. "I didn't mention this before, but they were spinning just like that with the other victims."

Tom took a closer look. "I wouldn't overthink it."

"Don't they look strange to you?"

"Not really. Flies do all sorts of crazy things. You ever see them rubbing their little hands together?"

Kani massaged her head. "He's moving fast, Tom. Hal or not, he's moving fast. This guy's been planning this for a long time. We need to catch up."

"I know," he replied. "Look, you should rest up. The station is on the other side of town. Why don't you leave your truck there tonight? I'll drop you off and pick you up tomorrow."

Kani hesitated at the suggestion, but couldn't think of a reason not to carry out the idea. She nodded.

As they were leaving, Tom stepped back and examined the body from a distance.

"What are you thinking?" she asked.

"Oh, I don't know. Just the whole . . . pilot, air, suffocation thing. It's—"

"Kinda genius?"

"Yeah. But let's not praise a cold-blooded killer."

Kani spent all evening anticipating the next murder. At this rate, if she couldn't figure out who the next victim would be, they'd be dead the next day.

Around seven, her mother called for her as she was getting out of the shower.

"Your phone's ringing!" she shouted from the recliner.

"I know!" Kani yelled back. "If I can hear you, I can hear it!"

She wrapped a towel around herself as she rushed to her bedroom.

"Guess who?" the voice on the line said.

"Gil."

"Why don't you sound happy? I'm calling ya, like you said."

Kani rolled her eyes. "What is it?"

"No plumbers."

"Damn. Servicemen? Anything at all?

"All service people are employed by the airport. No outside companies. But I'll call Westside tomorrow to get an idea of what Darnell's day looked like."

"Fine."

"You're welcome."

She hung up on him.

The next morning, Kani stood outside as she waited for Tom to pick her up. A dozen newspapers were scattered across their driveway, old and new. She'd gotten too lazy to toss them.

She walked over to the newest one, still crisp and, unlike the others, its ink hadn't bled from the wet weather.

That's when she saw the headline.

"Shit."

When Tom arrived, she almost forgot the uneasiness she'd felt yesterday and shoved the paper into his hands.

"They gave him a name?"

"It's fitting, I suppose," Kani replied. "But now he knows we've figured out his pattern."

Tom began reading the first paragraph. "'The Element Killer struck again yesterday afternoon when a female pilot was found strangled in an airport bathroom.'"

"Why can't they just say 'pilot'?"

"I don't believe the death has even been reported to the family," Tom noted. "How'd the info leak?"

Kani sighed. "Keep reading."

"'This is the third murder that has occurred in the past seventy-two hours. People are beginning to question the decision Chief Trumen Price made two years ago when he—'"

Tom folded up the paper.

"Why'd you stop?"

"Look, forget that," Tom said as he threw the paper onto the dashboard. "Are you taking care of yourself? Have you been eating?"

"The article mentions me, doesn't it?"

Tom ignored her question. "Hey, it's Tess's fourth birthday this Saturday. We're having a little party. We'd love it if you'd come."

"Gosh, Tom. Why didn't you tell me sooner? I don't have a gift."

"Ah, she'll have plenty. She just wants to see you. Please?"

That's when Kani remembered the way Tonya had looked at Tom.

"I don't know," she said. "I'll have to see."

Tom sighed and started the engine. "All right, Victur."

He didn't look at her or speak the entire drive.

At the station, Chief Price was up in arms over the article. He warned everyone on the team not to speak to anyone, even if they weren't journalists. "Not your sister, not your brother, not your dentist's wife's fucking cousin!"

Then, when a young sergeant used the name "The Element Killer," Chief Price slapped the bagel out of his hand and threatened to stick it somewhere distasteful if he heard that phrase again.

Once Sergeant Gil confirmed with Westside that Darnell had an alibi, Kani spent the day combing through the list of servicemen employed by the airport. She noticed that people sneaked glances at her all day, most likely because of whatever had been said about her in the paper.

Tom spoke to her only once, when he informed her that lunch had arrived.

Late Saturday night, Kani sat in the living room eating a Swanson TV dinner while her mother flipped through channels.

"They keep showing reruns," her mother complained. "I've seen all these."

Kani looked down at the aluminum tray in her lap. She had avoided going to Tess's birthday, and she wondered how disappointed Tom must be. She'd told herself she had to spend the day doing things for her mother, like picking up her Diet Coke and making her meals for the week.

Still, the guilt was eating at her. Tom might have acted standoffish, but this was someone with whom she'd spent the majority of her time with for the past two years.

She shook her head like she could disperse the thoughts and tried to distract her mind with something else.

"Have you heard from Keyla?" Kani asked.

"Not since she left," her mother replied. "She came to see me the day before."

"How did it go?"

"How do you think it went?"

Kani played with the green beans on her tray. "She'll be okay," she said, though she wasn't sure if she was reassuring her mother or herself.

"We interrupt this broadcast with breaking news."

Kani turned her attention to the blaring television. Her mother coughed and shifted in her seat.

"Mayor Akida has been reported missing. Officials say she was last seen on Thursday at a campaign event, but did not return home that evening. Her husband is asking the public to come forward with any information. We are told there will be a reward for—"

Suddenly, a fly landed on the camera lens, spinning as it blocked half the reporter's face. By the time a giant hand swatted it away, Kani's throat had already closed.

"It's him," she said, dropping her fork onto the tray. "It's our guy. I know it."

She stood and handed her mother the barely touched meal. "Here. Have this. I gotta go."

"What are you going to do?" her mother asked, still coughing.

"I don't know, but I have to find them before it's too late."

Kani shoved her gun into her holster. She started to head out the door when she stopped.

Fire . . . water . . . air . . .

"Earth."

She grabbed the phone hanging in the kitchen and dialed Tom's. She hoped he wasn't angry with her. She'd have to trust that her partner was the man she'd always known.

It rang five times before the machine answered. *"You've reached the Pertrans. It's Tom. And Holly. And Tess! Leave a message after the beep."*

"Tom," she said, "he has the mayor. I'm headed to the Doe Creek lot. Meet me there."

The lot was an eerie mound of dirt with no streetlamps to illuminate it. In the center was an incomplete apartment building, covered with plastic sheeting swaying gently. Mayor Akida had halted construction when she was elected, and no one could agree on what to do with it now.

Kani parked her father's truck across the street, pulled out her gun, and crept toward the building.

With her back against a wall, she peered behind a plastic cover. She spotted a small light inside and heard the faint sound of a woman whimpering.

Her gun leveled, Kani tiptoed toward the light, straining her eyes in the darkness.

When she got close enough, she could see fresh dirt lit by a single flashlight placed on the ground. But it wasn't the light that stunned her.

The dirt was moving, as though someone was fighting to reach its surface.

Kani dropped to her knees, slipping her gun back into its holster, and started to dig with her hands, sweating as she pushed more and more dirt behind her.

"I got you!" she shouted as she bore into the ground. "Keep trying!"

Fingertips touched hers. "Yes! Hang on!"

She pulled with all her might, not allowing herself to stop until she could see Mayor Akida's face emerging from the earth.

Just as Kani was about to free her, she saw the mayor's eyes widen followed by a loud clang. It took a moment for Kani to realize it came from right behind her.

Everything went dark.

Kani's head throbbed when she woke. She was in a chair, hands tied behind her back. Her holster was missing, and her badge glinted against a single flashlight set to its highest power.

As her vision began to unblur, she could make out the tiny familiar figure.

"Tonya?"

She could see her clearly now—white dress covered in dirt, blue heels, red lipstick.

"See. That's the thing," Tonya said, leaning her weight on a shovel. "I'm invisible to men, I know that. But what drives me insane is that I'm invisible to women like you. You're all a bunch of fucking hypocrites."

Kani squinted at the patch of dirt beside Tonya. Bile rose up her throat. She had failed to keep the mayor alive.

Tonya dragged the shovel across the ground, producing a streak in the dirt as she walked over to another chair. She leaned the shovel against the wall and sat down, her purse on her lap.

"I love my husband. He provides for us," she told Kani. "Every morning, we have breakfast together as a family. Then he goes to work his first house of the day while I walk the kids to school. I clean our home and tend to the garden. Around noon, I take a long nap before picking up the boys. Hal comes home around five. He's tired, but he still takes a moment to kiss me. After supper, once the boys are in bed, he gives me a foot massage while I ask him about his day. He thinks I'm just being a curious, doting wife. He doesn't know he's giving me a list of potential victims."

She took out a compact from her purse, reapplied her lipstick.

"Then he snores like a porker. A tornado couldn't wake him. Well, it helps that I crush sleeping pills into his food."

She laughed and put the compact away.

"That's when I make sure the boys are asleep, too. The house is so quiet." She gazed at the wall before turning back to Kani with chilling eyes. "But I'm quieter."

Kani swallowed. She wasn't sure where Tonya was going with this. She needed to stall so Tom could find her.

"How'd you kill the pilot?"

"Oh, that was easy," Tonya boasted. "She only flies domestic flights. They don't let her fly international. Figuring out her schedule didn't take long. I watched her go into the washroom and walked right in behind her. Nobody expects to die when they hear heels. She didn't see me coming at all."

"Why would she?"

"See, women like you and her are all the same. You're so high in the clouds, you don't see the rest of us down below. Get it? High in the clouds?"

"I did see you."

"As a victim. You felt *sorry* for me. You think my life is sad, but it's yours that's sad."

"Because I don't have a husband?"

"Because you don't know what your work is for."

Kani had the urge to kick her in the face. "To help people."

"People like *me*?" Tonya put on a baby voice. "Poor, abused wives who don't know any better? Ha! You didn't see me for what I really was."

"What are you, then?"

"The mastermind behind the murders you couldn't solve!" She cackled an extraordinary cackle, one that shook Kani to her core. "Have you been reading the paper this week? The people doubt your abilities, *Detective*."

"Those women were not the enemy," Kani answered. "If you were smart, you'd know that."

"If *you* were smart, you wouldn't be in that chair right now. Oh, the way I made you distrust your own partner—it was all too easy!" Her expression turned gleeful. "Now, look at you. Helpless. Would you like me to let you go, Detective? Then plead with me for it. Plead for your sad little life."

"My life isn't sad."

"No? Let's see . . . your father left you to have another family. You live with your mother, who requires your constant attention. You have no husband. Your sister's run off with hers, and the only friend you have is your partner, who has his own family to care for. I certainly wouldn't want to trade places with you. And yet, you pity me . . ."

Kani tried to block out the rest. Tonya was wrong. There was more to her life than the consequences of her father's actions. She was the first and only woman in her precinct. That had to mean something.

She wouldn't let Tonya get to her. Kani had done everything alone since her father left—she was capable. And she was fully capable of getting out of this.

But as she squirmed in the chair, the ropes around her wrist were tighter than she'd hoped. Her tongue was turning dry, and all she could think about was how desperately she needed Tom to burst in through the plastic sheeting.

Please, she thought. *Please be here.*

Tonya stood with her hands behind her back. She approached Kani—taking slow, calculated steps as her heels made marks in the dirt.

"They gave me a name, you know. 'The Element Killer.' It's not the best, but it'll be remembered."

When she got to Kani's chair, she circled like a buzzard, her voice coming from all sides.

"Fire. Water. Air . . . earth," Tonya gloated. "Pretty creative, don't you think?"

"You could call it that."

A fly landed on Kani's knee. She held her breath as she watched it spin.

"There's just . . . one thing missing," Tonya chimed, stopping in front of her.

Kani looked up, the realization hitting her like a truck.

Tonya showed her blackened teeth with a grin. She leveled Kani's own gun at her.

"Metal."

The Daylily Darling

The doctor lives atop the drumlin hill at the farthest edge of town. I am told he can fix anything.

"Anything?"

"Anything," the butcher claims. "I've seen men with clubbed feet prance out of there like wild horses."

He wraps the pink snapper in paper, coils string around the parcel, and hands it to me. I notice a splotch of blood on his chin. He looks me in the eyes—the only man to ever do so.

I tuck the parcel beneath my arm and push open the door, the bell clinking above my head. The December wind slices my cheeks. My coat grows damp from the snow. I press my chin into my chest and keep my view on my boots as I make my way down the sidewalk.

A body collides with mine. The parcel tumbles onto the ground and slides across the icy pavement.

"Oy! Watch where you're going, you halfwit!" grumbles a man. He's holding the gloved hand of a young schoolgirl, whose eyes widen as she looks up at me.

"Papa!" she exclaims. "Look!"

The man sees my face, his own turning pale. "Freak!" he spits. He tightens his grip on his daughter's hand and drags her away.

I loop my scarf around my face, covering what parts of my anomalies I could. The wool itches against my skin. Petals float to the ground. I pick up the parcel and head toward home.

I was born with a peculiarity, you see. Rumor has it that my birth mother's heart stopped the moment she saw me. From the neck down, I was as ordinary as any newborn. It was everything above it that took her that day.

Dunes scattered across my cheeks and forehead like cobblestones. Blemishes so dark, you might fall into them. Yet, my flesh was the least of her worries. It was what emerged from it.

Wildflowers.

That's right. Flowers, all colors of the rainbow, sprout from every mound upon my face. Poppies and daylilies and dandelions. Violets, nettles, and clovers. Stems and buds in all directions. My breath, their sun. My soul, their soil. It didn't matter how much they were nipped. They would sprout right back within seconds.

My widowed father left me under the ticket booth of an old stage theater—a wailing garden beneath a bundled blanket. The manager found me when she realized the faint sound came neither from the act nor the audience. A scribbled note told her to take me in.

Slush begins to seep into my worn boots. I would go to the doctor first thing in the morning, I decide. It would be a long trek up the mountainous hill.

The sky turns black in the short time it takes me to reach home. The marquee displaying the names of last night's acts illuminates the path to my front door. A Ragdoll cat purrs as it curls itself around my legs. I scratch behind its ears.

"I wish I could give you this snapper," I say. "But I'd sure be in trouble."

I unlock the glass entrance and hobble inside.

"Have you got it?"

"Yes, ma'am."

"Good."

Mother takes the parcel from my shivering hands and studies what eyes I have behind the bouquet.

"Did something happen again?"

"No. Why do you ask?"

"I know when you're lying, boy. I've raised you for twenty years."

She wanders toward the concession stand and unlocks the door hidden behind it. I follow her inside, where a burner stove sits beside a tub and a ragged sofa where Mother sleeps.

"Get the pan ready," she says to me as she unwraps the parcel in the sink.

I heave the large iron vessel off the shelf and place it on the stove. The wood-burning fire beneath it illuminates the kitchen. A fly lands on the butter dish, and I shoo it away as I slice off a knob and drop it into the pan. Mother slides the fish in. It sizzles, as does my chest.

I haven't told Mother of my plans to see the doctor. She wouldn't approve of such sorcery. Witchcraft, she'd call it. Yet was witchcraft not what brought me into this world? I see no other explanation for the curse I live with.

There was once a time I found my oddity precious. As a child, I never knew to despise the blossoms that grew from my cheekbones. As a matter of fact, I was quite fond of them. I'd stare into the mirror every day and keep track of the reds, the pinks, the purples. I'd pick at the blues and play with the yellows. Mother didn't treat my face any differently than she treated hers. She washed them both just the same.

It wasn't until I was introduced to civilization that I began to recognize it as an abnormality. For all of my youth, Mother only allowed me to venture into the outside world with her to the market. She did my schooling at home and never let me greet the theatergoers. She'd tell me to run the lights from the booth that hovered behind the audience. Often, I'd peer down at the eager faces before the show, trying to see what I could make of their loud whispers and animated murmurs.

Mother tips the pan over a plate. The fish slithers onto it.

After we finish supper, I head to the control booth. Its size is just enough to fit the lightboard as well as a cot we've had since I was a child. I let my body yield to the thin stained mattress, my shoulders nearly hovering over each side of the frame.

I would go to the doctor first thing in the morning.

"Get up!"

Mother tears the blanket off me. "'Tis daylight! What are you still in bed for?"

As I rub my eyes, a petal falls onto my pillow. I hadn't expected Mother to be up this early. She usually sleeps until she hears me churning butter for the popcorn maker of our concession stand. My visit to the doctor would have to wait.

"How am I to know it's daylight?" I groan. "There aren't any windows in here."

Mother goes over to the small dresser where I keep my clothes. "Let us get you in a clean shirt. We have a new performer arriving."

I sit up. "Why does it matter what I wear?"

"Because you're going to be doing the greeting."

"Me? Are you certain? Won't I frighten—"

She passes me a shirt. "You'll be just fine."

Half of an hour later, Mother hands me a bread roll and ushers me out to the lobby.

"Now, open the doors and wait for their arrival. I'll be backstage tidying the dressing room."

I notice she's sewn gold bugle beads onto the puffed sleeves of her ruby dress.

Mother senses my hesitation.

"It's early," she assures me. "No one will see you."

She disappears. I push open the doors, and the petals of my buds curl open the moment they're greeted by daylight. Outside, there is no movement other than the Ragdoll licking its paws beneath a table of the closed restaurant across the street.

I break off a piece of bread roll and fling it into the street. It lands in the snow a foot away from the cat, which stops its licking to crawl toward its snack.

Then comes the faint clicking of hooves. I gulp down the rest of the bread and brush the crumbs off my petals.

A carriage stops in front of the theater. The coachman steps off and turns the handle of the carriage door.

A man exits the vessel, the ends of his black mustache curving up toward the equally black top hat upon his head. The tails of his coat graze the step as he descends.

He tips his hat at me.

"Good morning, friend!" he calls.

I swallow as he approaches. "G-good morning," I say. "We are pleased to have you."

His eyes begin to examine every speck of pollen I possess, or so it seems. He grabs the edges of his open coat with both hands and tilts his head up at the marquee.

"Yes, yes. This will do nicely."

"What will you be performing, sir?" I ask.

He looks back at me. For a moment, I fear a remark about my face. Instead, he guffaws.

"Me? Oh, no! I'm not your performer."

He turns toward the carriage. The coachman extends his hand inside, and a delicate gloved arm emerges.

The tassels of her eggshell dress swing as she steps out. Her body never shivers despite not being dressed for winter. Her shoulders are bare and her legs absent of marks, but what strikes me most of all—what seizes the air from my lungs—is the cluster of wildflowers sprouting from her face.

"This is our star . . . Antoinette," the man says. "I'm her manager. Horace."

"I'm Aster," I reply.

I shake his hand, but my eyes cannot pull themselves away from Antoinette.

About my age, she peers at me with bashfulness from behind her inborn corsage and extends a hand. My heart is a racehorse as I kiss the fabric of the white glove.

"M-Mother is waiting for you inside. Allow me to take you to the stage."

I guide them through the lobby as they awe at the red carpet beneath their feet, the ornate chandeliers above their heads.

"It's smaller than other venues we've been to, but it's charming," says Horace.

"We do our best to care for it," I reply. "The wallpaper is new . . . we put it up ourselves."

A red lily twitches as Antoinette gives a hint of a smile.

I lead them to the house, where Mother had made sure to turn on the stage lights. The platform glows a golden yellow at the end of the darkness. We make our way down the aisle. Antoinette grazes her hand over the seats as we pass them.

When we reach the last row, Mother walks onstage from behind a curtain.

"Welcome to the Sam Harp Theater!" she trumpets. "Talented performers have graced this very stage for nearly three decades, from the renowned Agnes Gray-Bankes to Leon the Great!"

Horace raises both his arms. "Grand!" he exclaims. "What do you think, darling?"

Antoinette slowly makes her way up the steps. Her heels click lightly against the wood. Mother moves to the side, wringing her hands.

Antoinette stops at center stage and stares at the faint shapes of empty seats in the shadows. Her beauty is even more striking beneath the floodlights. Dew drops formed in the early hours glisten and wink upon her face.

She gives Horace a nod.

After Mother shows our guests the dressing room, Horace and Antoinette retreat to The Swann Hotel, where they'll be staying during the three nights of performances.

For the rest of the morning, I shovel snow in front of the theater. Mother shouts at me from the top of a ladder as she places letters onto our marquee.

"Tomorrow is opening night!" she tells me. "When you're done shoveling, type up the flyers and prepare the concessions."

My hair falls in front of my eyes as I dump the last of the frost.

"Why won't you just let me trim that mess?" Mother laments.

I push it behind my ear and rest the shovel on my shoulder. As I'm about to head inside, I realize I have yet to learn the name of Antoinette's act. Mother descends the ladder and puts her hands on her hips.

"Go on, then," she presses. "Get to the typewriter!"

I gaze up at the marquee.

The Daylily Darling

When evening comes the following day, a line of nearly eight dozen guests forms outside the theater. I had crafted many versions of the flyers before I was at last satisfied.

"Petals of Perfection"

"Bouquet of Beauty"

"A midwinter show of springtime"

"Stop and awe at the roses"

Eventually, I'd settled for *"Experience spring in midwinter!"*

"This looks promising," Mother says, peering behind the curtain of our ticket booth. "Go check on Horace and Antoinette. See if they need anything from our concession stand."

On my way through the lobby, I stuff a bag of peanuts in my pocket, knowing Mother and I will be forced to eat a late supper.

In the dressing room, Horace leans back in a chair, smoking a cigar. I walk in on him giving orders.

"No, no, that's too tight," he says. "Let some strands fall . . . like a fairy. Make her look as though she's just woken up in a bed of moss."

In front of the vanity, a beautician styles Antoinette's hair. I'm surprised to find her plucking the weeds from it so coolly, as though they are merely strands of gray.

"Evening, sir. Misses," I interrupt. "I've just come to see whether you'd like any refreshments."

Horace releases a puff. "A coffee would be grand. Fern?"

The beautician shakes her head.

"Antoinette isn't allowed sugar before the show," says Horace. "You got anything besides those bubbly drinks?"

"I can make tea, sir."

Antoinette peers at me through the glowing mirror in front of her.

"Chamomile," she says.

By eight o'clock that evening, every seat in the theater is filled. Chatter turns to hushed whispers that turn to silence as I lower the lights from the control booth. It is difficult to determine who is more anxious to see Antoinette perform—the audience or me.

I play the record Horace gave me. A thrilling tune I have never heard before begins to reverberate throughout the room. Instruments I have never known blare and blast, and I become so swept up in their sound that I nearly forget to click on the spotlight. Antoinette's silhouette is just barely visible on the stage. As soon as I light her, a soft gasp rustles throughout the crowd.

Are they in awe, or are they horror-struck?

I have not a moment to decide, for as Antoinette opens her mouth, the voice that resounds stops every beat inside my chest. It is ethereal . . . otherworldly, pure. She begins to dance about the stage, spreading her arms and pointing her foot high toward the ceiling. I light her as she moves, urging myself to keep up with her wild.

She is both a luscious garden and a boundless mare—a sensational force I could be in only my most radical of dreams.

Each song Antoinette performs is more entrancing than the last. She achieves four costume changes: a seductive jeweled dress, a flowing canary skirt paired with dripping pearls, a royal-blue evening gown, and an ensemble made of moss and peeling bark.

When the last note ends, I shut off the spotlight. The audience roars in the darkness. I move the controls of the lightboard, illuminating each color on Antoinette's face.

She begins to blow kisses to the crowd, and suddenly, mud plagues my chest. So many evenings I'd walk the cobblestones of the city I called my home only to reap pebbles thrown at me by wicked schoolboys. Now, I watch as the crowd throws coins and gifts at my parallel.

What do they see in her that I do not possess? Is it the way her purple hues complement the gold of her curls? Is it the lack of thorns upon her roses, or the abundance of leaves against her peonies? Perhaps it is the way she carries herself so delicately, as though standing on the tips of her toes.

Shame fills me as I realize my thoughts. Mother has always warned me that envy is a dangerous state in which to dwell.

I remain in the booth as the crowd dissipates, crunching on the last few peanuts left in my pocket. When no soul is left in the house, I begin swaying, mimicking what movements I remember from Antoinette's performance.

She startles me when she appears at the opening of the booth.

"I wanted to thank you before we depart," she says. "A girl can't be a star unless someone lights her."

Embarrassed, I cease my dancing and brush the salt from my fingers.

"Your performance . . ." I manage. "You were . . . extraordinary."

She chuckles and enters the booth. My racehorse returns.

"You're too kind."

"And that voice . . ."

"Geneva Bow. Isn't she sensational?"

"Who?"

"The singer." Antoinette reaches over to the record Horace gave me and holds it up. "The first time I heard her, I fell absolutely in love."

"You mean that wasn't your singing? Won't the audience be cross if they find out?"

"Find out? Everyone knows Geneva Bow. Haven't you heard of her?"

Her eyes dart around the meager room and stop at the cot where I rest.

"You don't leave the theater very much, do you?"

She gives a smile—one filled with more pity than I'd prefer.

"They're not here for my voice," Antoinette tells me. "You'd know that better than anyone."

"There you are! Dinner was ready half an hour ago."

Mother gestures to the plate of baked chicken and peas on the table as she cleans her own finished dish in the sink. I sit and begin cutting into the meat.

She turns to look at me as she dries the dish. "Were you with Antoinette?"

I nod and chew without looking up.

"What did she want?"

"Nothing," I mumble. "She thanked me."

Mother puts the dish away and removes her apron. She plops down into the chair across from me as I move my fork, creating the shape of a star with the peas on the plate.

"She's a nice girl, isn't she?" Mother remarks.

"I suppose."

She pauses. "I know my keeping you in here has deprived you of peers."

I look up at her.

"Is that why you invited her? For me?"

Mother adjusts herself in her seat.

"Aster," she says tactfully, "I won't encourage you to marry if your heart does not desire to. Hell, you know I never married. But I won't be around forever, and when that day should arrive, I should like to know that you'd have some sort of company."

I let my fork clatter onto the plate.

"Did Horace and Antoinette agree to this arrangement?"

"No, of course not! They're here for the performances, is all."

I rise from my chair, eager to be alone.

"You're not going anywhere until you finish your plate," says Mother.

On the second night, we sell a dozen more tickets than we did on the first.

I wander into the dressing room an hour before the show. Antoinette had left her ensembles for her performances on the garment rack. I make my way to the first gown, black as night, and run my fingers across the jewels of the bust, grazing the emeralds, diamonds, and garnets that shine like stars against the lit bulbs of the vanity. I caress the billowy fabric, admiring its quality, the way its weight slips through my hands. I wonder how it must feel to have that weight fall on my own figure—how the jewels would gleam against my own skin. Would the satin embrace my waist the way it does hers? Would it float as I dance?

I glance at the empty doorway before taking the dress off its hanger. With haste, I drift over to the long mirror beside the vanity. Pressing the sleeves against my shoulders, I let the garment fall in front of me, surveying the reflection that stares back. It is as though this royalty has been there all along— hiding behind a body bestowed to me that I never asked for.

"Hello."

A lump rises in my throat.

"I-I apologize . . ." I sputter, rushing the dress back to its hanger.

Antoinette shuts the door behind her. I fear I've destroyed the rapport we've developed. I would certainly not blame her for finding me improper.

Instead, she walks over to the rack. She lifts a delicate hand and rubs her index finger over the large center emerald.

"Exquisite, isn't it?" she says. "Would you like to try it on?"

I assume I've misunderstood her, but as she moves behind me and peels off my coat, I hear the howls and groans of betting men as the racehorse of my heart crosses the finish line.

Antoinette places my coat on the vanity and strips the gown off its hanger.

"Go on," she assures me. "It's all right."

I stare at the garment being held out to me. Is it a cruel trick? What does she hope to gain from such a request?

"There's no need to be afraid," she says, reading my mind's shadows.

"I–I couldn't—" I tell her. "I'll tear it . . ."

"Oh, nonsense. You're a frail little thing. Besides, Fern is as wonderful a seamstress as she is a hairdresser."

She takes my hand and places the collar of the dress within my grasp. Then she turns around, offering privacy. I find my feet nailed to the ground for a moment before I manage to place the dress down gently on the vanity chair. Slowly, I unbutton my shirt.

"I design all the pieces," Antoinette says with her back to me. "And Fern makes most of them."

My hands shake as I pick up the dress and unzip it. I put one leg into it, then the other. The satin is cool against my skin as I thread my arms through the openings.

"May I turn?" asks Antoinette.

"Yes."

Antoinette spins herself around and gasps. "The color! It's magnificent on you! Look in the mirror."

"Mirrors haven't always been my friend," I tell her.

"I noticed you didn't have one in that booth of yours. Give it a chance. I promise this time, it'll be kind."

I take a deep breath before turning toward my reflection. Antoinette places one hand on my shoulder blade and zips up the dress with the other. I swallow what words I have as the fabric gradually hugs my waist.

Antoinette's promise remains true. Jet-black fabric enlivens my skin, giving spotlight to the hued blossoms upon my face. The skirt's length grants me height, elevating both my frame and poise. And the jewels—the jewels pressed against my chest begin to absorb every affliction I have felt in my soul since the day I was born.

"Can you dance in it?" asks Antoinette.

This night, I am even more eager to watch Antoinette's performance. I admit my envy has not completely made its exit, but it is braided with adoration after our interaction in the dressing room. Any traces of green within me are merely for her grace, her fearlessness, and the control she holds over a crowd.

She entertains just as much as she did opening night, embracing each song as though it is the last time the world will hear it. All is well until the last ballad when a shout booms from the crowd.

"Devil!" a man spits.

Fear courses through me as I bring my attention to Antoinette onstage, who continues to twirl, paying him no mind.

"Abomination!" the man continues.

The crowd begins to grow louder. I cannot tell whether they are yelling for him to cease or joining in his repugnance.

Antoinette clenches her jaw, though she does not stop moving her body. The outlines of Mother and Horace appear in the aisle, searching for the source of the commotion. I do the only thing my mind can conjure amid the chaos.

I click on the spotlight and shine it directly on the man. He thrashes as people hold him back. Horace drags him out while Mother calms the rest of the audience members. Antoinette finishes her performance, but the crowd's applause feels disturbed and distracted. I search for signs of discomfort from Antoinette as she bows, but her coolness appears unshakable.

She visits my booth again when the theater proves itself empty.

"I brought you something," she says as she hands me a box.

I place it beside the lightboard. As I lift the lid, I am greeted with the tassels of a ravishing turquoise dress.

"I sent Fern out to grab it during the show. I hope you like it."

I close the box and place it in the top drawer of my dresser. "It's beautiful."

"I've sent Horace back to the hotel," says Antoinette. "Do you mind if I stay here awhile?"

She unbuttons her coat, revealing a lilac nightgown underneath.

"Are you hungry?" I ask. "My mother could make you supper."

Antoinette sits on the cot with one leg crossed over the other, leaning back with her palms pressed into the mattress behind her. She lifts her chin toward the wall shared with the lobby. "I think I'm craving popcorn."

The chandeliers of the lobby have been switched off, so we wander in the gloom. Mother's door is open just a crack—a thin ray of light piercing the concession stand. I know she is listening.

"Are you all right?" I ask Antoinette as I scoop popped kernels into a bucket.

Antoinette leans over the booth with her elbows on the counter.

"Oh, that ol' prick in the audience? I'm used to it."

Her flowers close slowly in the dark.

I pour butter over the overflowing bucket. "You mean it happens often?"

She snatches a kernel and plops it into her mouth. "Of course. Doesn't it happen to you?"

We make our way back to the house, where Antoinette skips down the aisle. Her nonchalance leaves me speechless as I stand clutching the bucket.

"Tell me when to stop," she tells me.

"Stop."

"Row twenty-seven," she says. "Tell me when again."

She squeezes herself through.

"Stop."

"Seat thirty-one!" she exclaims before plopping into the chair.

I follow, attempting to keep kernels from falling as I settle into the seat beside her. She grabs a handful and stuffs it into her mouth.

"These things don't maim me anymore," she continues. "I've had enough of it all."

"I don't understand how you do it. Where do you find that power?"

Antoinette looks down. "My folks . . . they weren't bad people, but they didn't know what to do with me."

She gazes at the stage. "Horace found me drinking my sorrows and took me under his wing. I would be on the streets without him. Or worse."

Her hand goes back into the bucket. "When you get a second chance at life," she explains, crunching at her dinner, "you don't let any brutes get in your way."

She stops.

"I'm not keeping you, am I? Is your mother waiting on you?"

I shake my head. "No. She—she wants us to become acquainted. She has this idea in her head that we should be married."

There is silence. Then, Antoinette lets out an irresistible laugh.

"Oh, dear," she snickers. "She has it all wrong, doesn't she?"

"I'm afraid so."

Antoinette turns to me.

"Aster. May I be frank?"

I nod.

"Your mother seems like a nice woman, but her keeping you in here has made you believe you don't deserve to be seen."

She looks beyond the wilted poppies around my eyes.

"You've been backstage your entire life. When will you make your entrance?"

Antoinette stands and buttons her coat over her nightgown.

"I had better go," she says. "Mother will scold me if I arrive back at the hotel so late in the evening."

"Mother?"

"Oh. That's what I call Horace," she explains.

I stand with her. "I'll walk you out to the carriage."

She chuckles. "Perhaps I *should* marry you."

The winter air has grown ten degrees colder since the first night of her performance. I rush Antoinette through the chill, and she scurries into the carriage. Before I shut the door, I hand her the popcorn bucket.

"For the road."

She blows me a kiss. As the coachman pulls the reins and the horse trots away, I notice the Ragdoll across the street again. It's huddled between two trash bins, nearly covered in frost.

I rub my arms and hurry toward the cat. It meows as I pick it up.

Once I'm back inside, Mother appears from her door behind the concession stand.

"If any theatergoers discover that thing in here," she says, "it goes back outside. Understood?"

I nod.

"Your hair's getting long. Come. I'll trim it for you."

I clutch the shivering Ragdoll to my chest.

"No," I say, turning my back to Mother. "Leave it."

On the third night, Horace greets me in the booth after Antoinette's last song.

"Our star has requested your presence at dinner with us this evening," he says. "Please meet us at the restaurant across the way whenever you're ready."

I wait until the crowd clears before exiting the theater. It is the whitest night of the year. The cold has chased most people back into their homes.

In front of the restaurant, I find myself hesitating. I've looked inside its glass hundreds of times, yet never entered. I've always wondered what it would be like to be surrounded by friends, chatting about the latest film or who's been seen with whom with no worries to bury us. Now, I fear whether I even have anything to contribute.

I walk in, and the noise dissolves. Diners drop their forks and chews become stares.

Finally, Horace rises from a table.

"Don't just stand there!" he shouts at the waiters. "Fetch some wine!"

I feel a hand against my back.

"Don't you mind these people," Antoinette says to me. "They'll be spilling coins to see you soon enough."

We join Horace at the table.

"What do you mean?" I ask.

"We have a proposition for you," Antoinette starts. She straightens her back. "Come with us on our tour."

I scratch at a nettle. Pollen falls onto the table. "Join you? As a technician?"

Antoinette giggles. "No, silly."

Horace places his elbows on the table. "As a performer."

I clear my throat. "A—a performer?"

"I'm told that you're a dancer," he replies.

Antoinette grabs my arm with both hands.

"We'll perform together. You could be . . . the Violet Vixen! Or we could be a matching duo: the Daylily Darlings!"

I lean back, trying to envision the unimaginable invitation they have bestowed. I cannot deny my excitement as I attempt to piece together the image of myself onstage. For so many years, I have danced alone in the privacy of the booth. Could I claim my nature was one primed to do so for the world?

The waiter fills the silence by bringing us a bottle.

"Take tonight to think about it," says Antoinette. "We are leaving The Swann at eight o'clock tomorrow morning."

We spend hours drinking wine and scarfing down devils on horseback and mapping out what a show featuring two budding stars would look like. By the time we finish, it is nearly midnight, and the roads have emptied themselves of life.

"You'd be a sensation!" Antoinette calls out to me from their carriage.

I watch them leave. The trot of their horse fades, and soon, the quiet embraces me.

The snow wraps round the ankles of my boots as I cross the street, brimming with elation after learning of boundless possibilities. My foot touches the curb only yards away from the theater when it skids across the ice. I am thrown onto the ground as my face hits the cobblestones. My forehead begins to ooze with warmth.

I attempt to straighten myself, but my vision grows dizzying. I hear the door of the restaurant open, and as I squint toward it, I see the blurry form of one of the waiters staring at me. I seek his aid through my gaze but am quickly left with a knot in my stomach when he turns back inside and shuts the door.

Thereupon, I am left alone, petals crusted with blood.

As I lie there, waiting for the inferno in my head to subside, I come to recognize I can only depend on myself to offer my existence any tenderness or humanity. I shall not transcribe others' conduct by being cruel to mine own soul.

They despise me for the fear within themselves—for the seeds they swallow that will not sprout. They wonder where I find water—how I keep these parts of me alive in the dead of winter. When they rest their heads on the flatness of their pillows, they dream of having the softness of foliage caress their cheeks. They walk on embers of lies, while I bathe in pools of truth.

I gaze up at the falling powder, glinting like specks of ambition within a hopeless grave. It is now that I begin to pity those who despise me—to bemoan the ropes that bind their hands to order and submission, for I have released myself of this confinement. I will no longer let the regulations of frightened characters dictate my own. I am a splash of color under black skies. I am woman. I am dreams. I am song.

Mother finds me crumpled up in a blanket of slush.

In the lobby, she pulls a handkerchief from her bosom and dabs my split lip as the cat coils itself around my legs.

"That thing's been waiting for you all night," Mother says.

"I've named her Sylvia," I tell her. "You're up late."

"Too anxious to sleep. Horace informed me of your dinner. I hope you turned down their offer."

"I haven't told them yet, but I've decided to accompany them."

I follow her into the kitchen, where she sits me down at the dining table. Sylvia jumps onto the sofa. Mother shoos her and begins to bandage my forehead.

"People aren't ready to see you," she says.

"I don't care."

"You don't know what they'll do to you, boy!"

My heart becomes a violent refrain.

I align my eyes with Mother's. "I'm going away with them."

She takes my chin and turns it toward the room's single lamp, studying the scrapes and gashes upon my face.

"I know it isn't easy lighting a stage for others to walk on, but it's what you need to do until the world changes."

She strokes the long strands of my hair. "You'll get your flowers one day."

I wrap my palm around her wrist, lowering her hand.

"I am flowers, Mother."

Sylvia meows from beneath the table.

The doctor lives atop the drumlin hill at the farthest edge of town. At six o'clock in the morning, I stand before his door as the tassels of my dress sway in the wind.

"Good morning, ma'am," he greets me.

"I am told you can fix anything."

He looks at my face.

"You're here about the posies, I presume."

"Yes," I answer. "I want more of them."

Shut Me Up in Prose

They shut me up in Prose -
As when a little Girl
They put me in the Closet -
Because they liked me "still" -

—Emily Dickinson

I blew up a hundred balloons and let them out onto the ocean. They were pink and orange and yellow, and by the time I was done the sea was covered with these wondrous floating orbs. The waves pushed the balloons up and down like ballerinas dancing in prismatic rhythm. The sun peeked through endless clouds, offering the perfect spotlight.

Clyde found me with sand in my hair and glass between my toes. When he saw what I had done, he gave me the look men often wear when they think you've gone mad.

Whenever Clyde gave that look, I could tell he thought he'd lost me forever.

Perhaps I was mad. Did it matter, if I had created something beautiful?

Every day, it's something, said Clyde.

I had hoped he would see the value in my design. I desperately longed for him to praise me like he did his colleagues, to think of my soul as something other than a shipwreck.

He yanked my arm.

Come inside before someone sees you.

I refused. He threw his arms around my waist and tossed me over his shoulder. I tried to scream, but I had already given my breath to the sea.

Instead, I pounded at his back.

One, two, black and blue.

When I grew exhausted, Clyde carried me to our bed. He fetched a towel and sat by my feet, removing a shard of glass as I winced.

You know better than to go barefoot out there.

I leaned over and yanked the towel from his hand. Through Clyde's affection always seeped hints of belittlement. There were worse things than a few cuts.

I thought it'd be different in a new town, he continued.

I plucked a shard from my heel.

Can't you shop for dresses or have tea with the other women? Must you always attempt theatrics?

I told him the women in the town were strange, that they spoke in echoes. It felt like they were all the same person, that there was no way to differentiate them.

He moved closer and brushed the hair from my eyes.

They're happy, that's why. They can't be bothered over anything beyond their homes.

He attempted to kiss my nose. When I turned away, he let out a sigh.

Listen, Roger told me of a place. Those who have come out of it are doing well. His wife, Helen, has been there herself. Perhaps it'd be good for you.

I knew what place.

It was a mile from our beach house. You could tell the building used to be blue before the ocean salt turned it gray. The walls displayed symmetrical windows, many of which faced the sea. The roof's shingles curved like waves, though the most charming feature was the glass pane within it, glimmering as it faced the sun. The structure was grand in its size yet quaint in its design. At first glance, it seemed like a dwelling one could dream of residing in.

Yet, the most notable detail of all was that it stood at the bottom of a very large pit of dirt.

I got a better look, once, when Clyde ran over a nail and pulled off to the side of the road. He had inspected the tire, muttering endlessly about wasted time, while I wandered to the edge of the high road above the building.

It was then that I noticed the pair of black steel doors at the front, rusting at their bolts, while the windows alongside them held silver bars. The paint on the walls peeled like sunburned skin, and the roof was studded with the droppings of crows.

I thought perhaps someone's poor home had slid down amid a mudslide, but Clyde told me it had been built within a hole on purpose. When I asked why, he simply told me to fetch the jack from the trunk. Whatever the reason, I decided it was a place I never wanted to go.

I tossed the last shard of glass onto the nightstand, a delicate clink against the wood.

Clyde got to his feet and spoke.

I don't know what to do with you.

Roger and Helen lived in the beach house just a little ways from ours.

I had only met them once, at one of Clyde's work parties. I never liked those outings, as I felt they stifled everyone in constant competition. I remembered Helen vividly, however. She would make her way around the room in a beige dress, holding a bottle of whiskey and offering to fill the businessmen's glasses. I noticed she took her time, pouring casually as her ear turned toward their conversations. I was drawn to her. She was different, like she knew something others did not.

I decided to pay her a visit. I knew she would be alone, with Roger at the office. She was startled by my presence, using the door to shield her body as she opened it.

Hello, said Helen. *Is something the matter?*

I apologized for my intrusion and told her I was the wife of Clyde, a friend of her husband's.

That's right, yes. What can I do for you?

I asked if I could talk to her about the pit.

She remained composed. *What pit do you mean?*

I explained how Clyde had told me she had spent time there.

I must go now, she said. *I've left a chicken in the oven.*

I pleaded for her time, told her I was afraid they'd send me to it. She glanced behind me, as if to check whether anyone else was around.

Just be who they expect you to be. Not many of us make it out.

She shut the door before I could say another word.

Daunted, I wandered back. The spray of the sea kissed my face as I considered whether to tell Clyde that I had seen Helen. He'd be thrilled in a way that irritated me, hoping Helen would have moved me to be more like her. He'd bring up how she doted on Roger and praised every little feat, even drafting sketches for her husband to present at work.

With your ideas and my pitches, he'd tell me, *we could outshine them.*

I decided not to mention the visit.

When I arrived home, I was surprised to see the car outside. I found Clyde in the midst of stuffing a suitcase, scurrying around all corners of the bedroom. I thought at first he was leaving me until I realized the items were mine.

I ran to the washroom. He went after me. I slammed the door before he could reach me, locked it as he pounded. I had made Clyde get rid of the window when we first moved in, after stepping out of the bath and locking eyes with a grinning gentleman taking a stroll on the shore. Now, I desperately longed for the freedom it would have granted me.

I collapsed onto the cold tiles, tears soaking my knees as I hugged them against my chest. There must have been something wrong with me, if so many thought the same. I was terrified of being reformed. My spirit lived by my madness. What would I become without it?

I could hear them on the other side when they arrived, differing voices but all with the same judgment. They tore out the knob. I screamed as the door swung open. Men in unassuming clothes lifted me by my arms, and I would have rather died than let them take me. I would have rather died than live in a hole.

I pounded at them harder than I'd ever hit Clyde.

One, two, one, two.

They forced me out the washroom, pulled me through the house to the front door.

Only for a little while, said Clyde, following close behind. *Please understand, darling.*

I spat in his face as they dragged me out. He stood in the doorway, wiping his cheek with the back of his hand.

I sought mercy in the face of the man who had carried me through the same doorway on our wedding night. The billowy layers of my dress had obstructed his view, causing him to stumble over the edge of the rug as we both toppled onto the couch. He had turned bright, laughing and laughing before picking me up again. Now, his face was sullen and tired. Some part of me felt every line that had formed was my doing.

They pulled me farther and farther as my vision began to blur. I could make out the porch we had built together, when he had taken a hammer to his thumb and whined like a child as I wrapped it in gauze. I gazed at the roof I used to climb on when he was asleep, hoping I could stretch my eyes beyond the ocean and marvel at the sensations on the other side.

I gave him one last pleading look. He stuck his hands in his pockets and offered me his back.

I woke to harsh bedsprings digging into my shoulder blades and the shadow of even bars on the wall across from me. My bare feet touched cold cement, reviving me as I hobbled toward the door.

Peering through the small square window, I could see an empty hall. I rattled the knob with both hands, pounding and kicking until a gentle voice said, *Don't worry, the matrons will let us out for breakfast.*

In my panic, I hadn't noticed the bed parallel mine on the other side of the room. There sat a girl with warm copper skin, rummaging through a pile of matchboxes. She seemed to be in the middle of placing them into rows.

I'm Seraphina, she said. *I'm so glad you're here. It was beginning to get a little lonely. Helen used to share this room with me, but they let her go.*

I asked for Helen's surname. Seraphina said they were never used here, so I asked whether Helen had a husband named Roger. Her eyes lit up.

Oh! You do know her! Is she well?

I admitted I had only met her twice, and that she hadn't told me anything about the place, or whether she was happy.

Seraphina scooped the matchboxes into a large cloth satchel and shoved them beneath her bed.

I could hear the faint rumbling of ocean waves behind the frenzied cawing of crows. I made my way to the barred window, and as my face desperately searched for sunlight, it dawned on me why they had built the place in a hole.

I asked Seraphina what the point of the bars was. She walked over to me, looking between them at the dry dirt walls that surrounded us.

Miss R likes to make sure this place resembles the world as much as possible.

The door clicked and swung open, revealing two expressionless women in lilac dresses and ivory aprons. They beckoned us into the hall.

Come, said Seraphina. *Let's get something in your stomach.*

She led me down the far-reaching hallway of amber walls and indistinguishable doors. The matrons unlocked each room one by one as other women slowly emerged. Two more matrons came down a flight of stairs with more residents behind them. There must have been eight dozen or so. I studied their faces, trying to gather which women had been there for days, months, or years. They never bothered to look at me, as though I had been there all along.

Seraphina grabbed my hand and pulled me through. *They don't give us long to eat. I'll introduce everyone during art.*

For breakfast, they served us figs and meatloaf and cranberry juice. We drank water from glass bottles that tasted like scum.

Afterward, we emptied our trays and shuffled back down the hallway to the main room. On one side, easels and canvases were accompanied by butcher paper and aluminum bins of paints. Tables with chess boards and books sat in front of a fireplace, while a single television set stood in the center of the room. The largest wall held the black steel doors, their presence reigning over the room, both threatening and seductive.

Seraphina walked me to the first resident, who was sitting in front of the television.

This is Elda. She's the strongest woman in the whole place, if not the whole world!

I eyed the gaunt, wrinkled soul in the rocking chair with plastic tubes in her nose. The tubes were attached to a bag hanging upon an iron stand, their transparency showing orange solvent crawling through them like earthworms. Seraphina pulled a piece of meatloaf out of her pocket and placed it in Elda's lap, carefully hiding it beneath her hands.

They don't let her eat, she said. *They thought her strength was too much. She's only allowed what's in the tubes, so I spare what I can. You won't tell?*

I shook my head, wondering how someone's strength could be too much.

Seraphina beamed. *She took down three grown men in a bar fight! Didn't you, Elda?*

Damn right I did, sweetheart, said Elda. *Then those bastards put me in here.*

Language, Elda, hushed Seraphina. *You know Miss R said to watch our mouths.*

She also said to watch my diet, mumbled Elda as she snuck a bite of meatloaf.

Seraphina led me to another woman in a corner of the room.

This is Vel.

Vel was staring at the wall, her hands tied to the arms of a wheelchair. Her limbs were covered with odd blemishes and scars creeping up as far as her shoulders and neck.

There's nothing wrong with her legs. The chair just makes it easier for us to move her. She has to stay tied down during art or she'll draw on herself.

Seraphina pulled a tube of lipstick from Vel's pocket. She straightened Vel's jet-black hair on her shoulders and applied the bleeding red upon her lips.

Miss R says ink doesn't belong on skin. Unless it's to paint our faces.

Vel twitched in disgust.

I'm sorry, Vel, said Seraphina. *The matrons will check that you have it on.*

She slipped the tube back into Vel's pocket.

Vel remained quiet, though she offered me a small smile. I looked at the scars across her body. They were purposeful, curling and weaving like vines, accompanied by blisters of blooming flower buds.

She didn't want to hurt herself, explained Seraphina. *She just wanted the designs, is all. They're beautiful, aren't they?*

Seraphina told me how none of the women knew exactly what they had to do to leave. They assumed they had to simply follow the rules, and if they followed them well enough, they'd be released.

Most of the women have been doing everything they've been told, she said. *But they're still here.*

A cluster of screams came from the hall, growing louder with each second.

Seraphina pushed me into the wall, running to the doorway as all four matrons carried in a howling, writhing girl by her limbs.

I WANT TO GO TO THE MOON, the girl shouted. *I WANT TO GO TO THE MOON!*

Seraphina took an armchair in front of the television and dragged it to them. The matrons thrust the girl into it.

I WANT TO GO TO THE MOON!

Seraphina bent down in front of her as the matrons held the girl tight.

Mirabel, said Seraphina. *Would you like to paint with me? We can paint the night sky.*

I WANT TO GO TO THE MOON!

Perhaps you could draw the moon, coaxed Seraphina. *And the stars.*

The girl twisted and squirmed. *I WANT TO GO TO THE MOON!*

Mirabel, we've told you. You can't go to the moon.

Mirabel thrashed even harder.

She's been at it all morning, said one matron. *We don't want to put her away again.*

Mirabel, please, begged Seraphina. *Don't you want to go outside today?*

Mirabel stopped and turned her head toward the windows. She kept silent.

The matrons looked at one another and let go. They raised their aprons, dabbing sweat from their foreheads. As they shuffled away, I noticed one slip a matchbox into Seraphina's pocket.

Seraphina placed a sheet of paper and a piece of charcoal into Mirabel's hands. Mirabel remained still, hardly blinking as she continued gazing at the window.

I remained pressed against the wall. Seraphina calmly made her way to an easel.

You'll get to know everyone in time, she said to me. *Would you like to paint something?*

I asked her what was wrong with Mirabel.

Seraphina dipped a paintbrush into a fiery red.

Same thing that's wrong with all of us.

Miss R was a robust woman with gray in her bun and shadows beneath her eyes. She wore a dusty-plum ensemble and sat behind a large pinewood desk.

We are very glad to have you here. You mustn't be angry at your husband. Many are sent here by their loved ones.

I opened my mouth to defend my fury, but she carried on.

These . . . showpieces you create, they attract unwanted attention. People can say cruel things about those with wild ideas. Your husband is protecting you.

She picked up a file from the desk, combing through the pages.

He tells me you once lived a charming life together. Then, over time, you grew sick of your routine, developed . . . ideologies, and began to exhibit erratic behavior.

She put down the file.

It seems your nature makes it difficult for you to function in our society. It is my goal to help you fix that.

I couldn't find words. In the silence, she offered a loving smile.

Did you enjoy meeting the other women in our residence?

I told her they were kind, but that I still wished to leave.

You are to stay until you're reconstructed.

She gave a signal to the matron, who carried in a metal cylinder and placed it on the floor beside me.

This is for you, said Miss R. *A welcome gift.*

I stared at the device.

It's a helium tank, she told me. *People blow up balloons with it, and they float in the air, where they belong.*

I looked at it, then back at her.

I'll have a basket of balloons sent to your room, she said. *I believe you have a preference for bright colors?*

I stood, knocking the chair over behind me and kicking the tank as it rolled across the floor. Papers fluttered around us as I tossed my file skyward and demanded my release, shouting about how I refused to live in a hole.

She never even blinked. *Then I suggest you cooperate.*

The mere sight of meatloaf eventually made me sick to my stomach, so Seraphina would take mine and offer me her figs. Mirabel would throw a fit after breakfast at least four times a week, screaming about how she wanted to go to the moon. Other times, she would sprint into the room and hop barefoot along every surface of furniture until the matrons forced her down.

The helium tank sat untouched on the floor at the foot of my bed, along with a basket of colored balloons. Seraphina told me we were all given gifts without direction, and she believed we were to use them as they were intended.

While the others spent time painting endless mountains and flower fields, I made note of every window and door I could find. I studied the kitchen behind the glass counter, along with the dining hall and the main room. I was able to observe the quarters on the second floor when a matron asked me to deliver porridge to a resident who had fallen ill. The upper rooms were more refined, and I learned later they were reserved for the matrons, as well as residents who were further along in their reformation.

There was a single door at the end of the matrons' rooms that supposedly concealed a stairwell leading to the third story. Seraphina told me it was where they kept Mirabel during her tantrums and, from what she knew, it was simply an attic.

I despised the washrooms. There were two on each floor at opposite ends of the hall, filled with numerous filthy stalls and showers. When I brushed my teeth on the first day, I nearly choked as I scooped the water from the sink into my mouth.

Oh, Seraphina had said as I spat and coughed. *The water here comes straight from the ocean, so be cautious not to sting your eyes. The only fresh water we get is during meals.*

Every day, Miss R would hold strange lessons in the dining hall. Sometimes she would ask us hypothetical questions, other times we were told to perform given scenarios. We played husbands and wives, businessmen and secretaries, barmaids and drunks. I didn't do well with my first performance as a stewardess, for when I made sure to enunciate, I was scolded for speaking too loudly.

After our lessons, they would let us go outside. I discovered the front doors stayed unlocked, which hardly made sense considering the barred windows. During this time, we would do stretches or stare up the walls of the deep pit we dwelled in. I would examine the outside of the building, counting its windows and determining which belonged to what room.

Whenever I looked up at the edge of the pit, I thought of Mother and Father, and whether they were shaking their heads as they watched me from the heavens.

What have you done, little sandpiper? I'd picture Father saying.

Then I'd go back to studying windows.

One day, as we were taking in the fresh air during our scheduled time outside, Mirabel began throwing a tantrum even Seraphina could not ease. She threw herself at the side of the pit again and again and again, screaming at the top of her lungs.

I WANT TO GO TO THE MOON, she wailed. *THE MOON, THE MOON, THE MOON!*

The matrons had been worn thin from an earlier fit and were ready to take her away. They tried to grab her, but she darted back and forth to different sides of the pit, launching herself against the dirt walls and caking her skin with dust.

THE MOON, THE MOON, THE MOON.

As they chased her, I had a sudden thought and bolted inside. I could hear Seraphina calling for me as I ran through the main room and into the hall, panting as I reached my quarters.

I grabbed a yellow balloon from the basket and ran my hands all over the helium tank, trying to figure out how to use it. I finally managed to stretch the balloon's opening over the mouth of the tank, turning the knob until I heard a hissing sound.

The balloon began to expand, then shot out in one swift motion, fluttering onto the ground. I tried again, this time holding the balloon in place. When it was glorious in size, I tied the end, fingers turning white from the attempt, and sprinted back outside.

The matrons had been able to catch Mirabel in the time I was gone, but they were having trouble dragging her toward the door.

I shouted Mirabel's name. Once, twice. Then I called for the moon.

Mirabel stopped squirming. The matrons immediately placed their hands on their knees, bending over to catch their breaths.

There was silence as Mirabel stared at the balloon held up by a pinch of my fingers.

I let it go.

It glided into the air and we all looked to the sky, watching as it drifted farther and farther. Mirabel stood frozen, eyes fixated on the speck, chest heaving in and out. When it shrunk from our sights, she looked at me. It was then I feared I must have done something awful, that she would come charging at me and scratch my face until it bled.

Instead, the centers of her eyes glimmered. She kept her gaze on me for a moment, then began her stretches with the others, to Seraphina's bewilderment.

After that day, Mirabel's tantrums grew less frequent, and only arose whenever the matrons seemed fairly rested.

In order for me to carry out an escape, I had to settle two things: how to unlock the door of my room without waking Seraphina, and how to climb out of the pit once I was outside. It didn't take me long to solve the former, for one night, as we made our way down the hall to bed, I watched as the matrons shut the door behind the residents. Not once did they use their keys in the process, at which point it dawned on me that the doors locked themselves.

When I was sure Seraphina was fast asleep, I tiptoed toward the door. The moonlight from the window beamed along the way as I peered through the crack. I observed it contained a simple lock, one that could be interrupted by jamming something into the doorframe. And, without the task of locking the door with a key, the matrons would hardly realize the difference.

I found the hole in the frame similar in size to Seraphina's matchboxes, so I stole one from the satchel and crawled back into bed, slipping it beneath my pillow.

I had a solution to my first dilemma but still had to sort out the latter. It seemed virtually impossible, which was doubtless why no one had ever attempted it. Little did I know, the solution would be presented to me, like another remarkable gift.

It happened one day when I was called into Miss R's office for my first monthly review. She was wearing her usual ensemble, though it seemed to have grown a dustier plum over time.

Have you been adjusting well? she asked. *The matrons tell me you're not interested in painting.*

I must have been influenced by Elda, for I answered cheekily and said I was more of a sculptor.

The corner of her mouth twitched. *I hear you've been using the helium tank.*

I told her I had only used it once, for Mirabel, and that I still wished to leave. She scribbled my words in a notepad.

Are you not fond of the place? she replied. *I created it myself. The men out there trust me, and that allows me to help us. You can do anything if people trust you.*

I argued that Elda should be allowed to eat and that Vel should be able to draw on herself. I said the meatloaf was awful and the salt water was beginning to burn my skin. Then I told her I hated how the windows gave the illusion we had any sort of freedom, while the bars said otherwise.

When I finished, Miss R looked me in the eye and said, *Would you like to work in the kitchen? Perhaps you could assist the matrons in preparing a better meatloaf.*

Oh, how thrilled I was. Seraphina would ask me to sneak more food that she could spare for Elda. I would hide an extra slice of meatloaf beneath her napkin, which I had improved by using the figs to make an accompanying sauce.

The matrons weren't much company in the kitchen. They had humdrum voices and focused on getting things done. We'd wash trays and boil seawater to separate the salt.

Miss R would arrive at the crack of dawn, the same time as the grocery delivery. The delivery man would prepare a pulley with a large wooden crate that she sat upon. She'd hold one hand on the rope and the man would turn on the machine, lowering her into the pit. I noticed she would always extend her legs to prevent her stockings from snagging on the wood.

When she reached the bottom, Miss R would make her way inside through the steel front doors. I'd help the matrons push a dolly out the kitchen door with a crate full of garbage from the day before. We'd switch the two crates, wheeling the crate of food through the kitchen to prepare breakfast while the pulley hoisted the other crate up and out of the pit.

One hazy morning, Miss R and the delivery man were late as the residents whined in the dining hall. The matrons were distracted by their attempts to shush them and hadn't noticed the delivery dropping in.

I was drying trays in the kitchen when I looked out and saw Miss R hop off the crate and shuffle to the front doors.

It was then I realized my freedom.

I looked over at the matrons, who were beginning to make their way back to the kitchen. There was hardly any time to act, and panic ran through me.

A ravenous howl echoed from the back of the dining hall. My eyes followed its source to discover Mirabel standing atop a table. She paused only to give me a sly look before curling her lips and continuing her cries.

Oh, Mirabel. Wondrous, brilliant Mirabel.

The matrons rushed to her. Without allowing myself the chance to hesitate, I pushed the old crate out, heaving and pushing as hard as I could and dragging it onto the platform. I heard a door slam as the delivery man climbed into his truck. I shoved the lid of the crate open, Mirabel's deafening wails fading as I climbed into the abyss.

The darkness swallowed me for what felt like decades. The smell was nauseating. I held my breath as I doubted my plan, remembering how Mother would scold me for my impulses.

You may have thought of X, she'd remark, *but you've forgotten about Y.*

The crane began to groan as I felt myself torn from the ground. For a moment, I wished I'd taken the helium tank with me, imagined breaking into the house with it and scaring Clyde half to death.

Light greeted me harshly as a hand gripped my arm.

Seraphina.

She tugged hard as I fought. The moving platform lifted her off her feet as she held on. The delivery man must have noticed the jiggle of the rope, for he looked down and began making a ruckus.

Seraphina looked up with a smile. *Apologies, sir! Just looking for a tray we threw out.*

She forced me out of the crate, wiggled her fingers at the man, and dragged me inside. As soon as we were in the kitchen, she answered my question before I even asked.

Mirabel never throws tantrums at breakfast.

I yanked my arm away.

It's worse out there than it is in here, she said. *You'll realize that with time.*

I shoved her, told her to stay out of my way. If it weren't for her, I'd be out already, running along the sand and bathing in the sea.

Did you really believe, she replied, *that after all these years, you're the first to attempt an escape? There isn't one. You're not smarter than the rest of us.*

Then she crept back to her table, and I knew not what to do other than rinse the waste scraps from my arms, my hope draining with the water.

I woke the following day to the door of our quarters swinging open.

Escape all you want, taunted Miss R. *They'll just send you back.*

She shut the door.

I glared at a waking Seraphina.

I didn't tell her, she insisted. *I swear. It must have been the delivery man.*

I placed my head on the pillow and turned my back to her, refusing to listen.

Please understand. I know Miss R seems wicked, but she does what's best for us.

I continued to ignore her, causing a strained silence between us. I could feel her hesitation, a wild flame desperate to ignite.

I used to be like you, she said, *fighting everything about our world.*

After a moment, I gave in and turned to face her. She was lost in her recollection, not bothering to look at me as her eyes searched the crevices of her memory.

I never wanted children, you see. But he–he forced it on me, and—

She erupted into tears.

I was just so terrified when I found out, I could no longer think properly. I wanted to be rid of it so badly, I–I thought I could burn it out of me. I know it was mad, but I didn't know what else to do! When I lost the baby, he blamed it on me . . . kicked me out of the house and turned everyone against me, even my mother.

I sat up and threw my legs over the edge of the bed, clutching the side of the mattress as I faced her. She took a breath and swallowed.

Miss R saved me by bringing me here. She told the matrons to give me a matchbox every time I obey their orders. When I collect enough matches, as long as none are lit, I'll get to become a matron here, too. I don't know what "enough" is, but I count them every day and tell her how many I have.

I was speechless, never having once considered anyone would be in the pit by choice.

It's easier when you don't have to fight anything, said Seraphina. *Miss R is better to me than anyone ever was. It's my fault a life is gone. At least nobody reminds me of that in here.*

Then she lifted her shirt, revealing the burns across her stomach, patches of red and white and anguish.

I rushed to Seraphina's side, taking her hand. I told her how she hadn't done anything wrong, that it was wrong for him to have forced it on her in the first place. I told her how she didn't need a child to be an astonishing mother, that she was wonderful to the other women, feeding Elda and comforting Mirabel and looking after me.

And as I thought of her words and the constant battles I had so tirelessly fought outside the pit, I found my desire to escape subsiding.

Seraphina threw her arms around me, and for a while, all was perfect and well.

It happened on a day as ordinary as any other. We had finished breakfast and retreated to the next room, except for Mirabel, who had been called into Miss R's office for her review. I was reading a book of poetry to Vel when Elda, who seemed to have grown stronger by the day, began to shout from in front of the television.

I'll be damned! she cried. *I don't believe it.*

The women all hurried over. I pushed Vel's wheelchair through the swarm. We stared at the screen, watching as a faceless man hovered across a pale desert floor.

That's one small step for a man. One giant leap for mankind.

Elda gasped. *They've done it*, she said. *They've really done it!*

Seraphina began to panic, running toward the television, attempting to shut it off as another resident fought her. *What are you doing?! This is history!*

M–Mirabel . . . stammered Seraphina.

But it was a moment too late. Mirabel had come back from her meeting, numbly walking into the room from the hall. Her eyes fixated on the screen as she made her way closer. She remained silent, and for a short while, I thought perhaps she was thrilled.

And then there was only a wash of sound. The excruciating scream, a violent wail as she fell to her knees. Mirabel howled, and Seraphina threw herself to the ground, holding her tight against her.

The matrons came running in, peeling Mirabel from Seraphina's arms (*No! I'm all she has. Please!*) and dragging her into the hall until her cries faded into silence.

Seraphina remained crumpled on the floor. I pushed through the others to help her up, stammering about how I didn't understand, that I thought this was good because it meant Mirabel was right, that she really could have gone to the moon.

But she didn't, whimpered Seraphina. *Because she's in here, don't you see?*

And then the women returned to their activities, chins lower than before as their eyes avoided the screen.

They didn't let us out for breakfast the next morning. The women pounded on their walls, shouting for the matrons. When our doors finally opened, they instructed us to head outside. As Seraphina and I shuffled down the hall, we saw Vel running down the steps from the second floor.

Seraphina, she whimpered.

It was the first time I'd heard her voice, piercing us with the words that followed.

It's Mirabel.

Seraphina darted for the stairs, knocking over residents along the way. I ran after her. When we reached the top, we could see the matrons and Miss R at the end of the hall. They were gathered in front of the third-story door, and I noticed it was ajar.

When she spotted us, Miss R made her way over, steps echoing as she crossed through the infinite stretch.

You are to go outside, ladies. Don't make me ask you again.

Please, Miss R, begged Seraphina. *Is Mirabel—*

Miss R remained silent before taking a breath.

You did everything you could for her, Seraphina.

I caught Seraphina in my arms as she seared my chest with every cry she gave. I glared at Miss R as the grueling sobs filled the air between us. It was then that I came to despise her, for if it were not for the pit, Mirabel would not be dead.

The women did nothing for days. No one felt like playing chess, or painting, or going outside. One morning, as we stared glumly at the television, a resident mentioned she'd heard Mirabel had jumped from the attic.

Nonsense, another said. *We would have heard the glass break.*

I heard she drank the saltwater, a third chimed.

No one could drink that much in a night, said a fourth. *She probably broke a bottle and cut herself.*

SHUT UP! ALL OF YOU! SHUT UP!

The women went silent. It was the first time Seraphina had spoken in days.

A matron waltzed into the room and made her way toward the fireplace. We didn't quite process what she was carrying, but once it was placed upon the mantel, we knew.

When the matron left, I followed Seraphina before the fireplace. She stared mournfully at the plain wooden urn.

She hated it here, said Seraphina. *And now she'll be here forever.*

I don't know how it came to me. The thought splashed into my mind like a gift from another world.

I rushed to the center of the room and switched off the television. The women turned their attention to me. I told them my plan, though I feared their responses.

There was a silence at first, and then,

Count me in, said Elda.

Me too, whispered Vel.

And me.

And me.

For Mirabel.

For Mirabel.

For Mirabel.

I looked to Seraphina, who hesitated before sprinting to the doorway. I half expected her to betray us to the matrons, but instead, she peeked her head into the hall before turning to us.

It's absolutely mad, said Seraphina. *But what can they do? We're already in here.*

We distributed Seraphina's matchboxes throughout a span of twenty-six days. Once each pair of residents had a box, we scheduled our plan for the night of a full moon.

The matrons shuffled us to bed, and we stuck the matchboxes into the pockets of the frames before they shut the door behind us.

When all was still, we crept out the hall and into the main room. We placed chairs beneath the knobs of the matrons' doors and gathered bottles from the kitchen. Then we took butcher paper and rolled it into cones, holding the pointed ends over the mouths of the bottles.

Seraphina removed the urn from the mantel and opened the lid. She approached each resident's creation, pouring a little into each cone as the ashes rained into the bottles like wistful hourglasses. I followed close behind, handing each resident a balloon as they stretched them over the bottles' mouths. We turned the bottles upside down and let the remains seep into the rubber pouches. One by one, I inflated the filled balloons with the tank, ashes swirling inside each colored globe as it grew.

An empty glass bottle clattered and rolled across the floor as the resident who knocked it over offered a look of grief. We held our breaths, staying still and silent.

Then came the rattling of doorknobs. We panicked, the women's hands shaking as they tied the ends of their balloons. I inflated the remaining ones until there were none left in the basket I'd been given.

The rattling turned into pounding.

We pushed open the steel doors and scurried outside, holding the tails of each orb by the tips of our fingers. The cold night air kissed our cheeks, and for the first time, the high dirt walls felt like a comforting embrace.

We heard the crash of a fallen door from inside the building. I asked Seraphina if she was ready. She eyed the glowing sphere above us, looked back at me, and nodded.

The matrons burst outside, and we sent Mirabel to the moon.

Miss R stood still behind her desk. I paced back and forth, emphasizing how I wasn't sorry and that she could lock me away for as long as she wanted to. I was simply honoring Mirabel's wishes. When she didn't answer, I accused her of being responsible for Mirabel's death, saying how she should have never locked her up in that attic.

Locked? said Miss R. *The door doesn't have a lock. The attic was the only thing that kept her calm.*

At that moment, I realized I never knew Mirabel's gift. I had always assumed her tantrums led to her being locked away. Now I pictured how the night sky must have looked through the charming glass pane.

Miss R opened her desk drawer and took out a document.

I was very impressed with your performance, she said, *using balloons that way.*

I was at a loss for words.

You did what was asked without losing the storm within you.

She scribbled her signature at the bottom of the paper.

It is time for you to go home.

I did not know what to feel. I told her I couldn't leave without the others.

The less of them out there, said Miss R, *the better for us in the long run.*

I pleaded for her to at least spare Seraphina.

Helen begged me the same. The tasks I give Seraphina prevent her from crumbling to ashes. They'd chew her up out there.

She folded up the document and slipped it into an envelope.

If you want to help her, you'll do as I say. Disguise your rebellion in obedience. Make them believe you are working with them even when you are not. It is your duty to represent us.

I protested. I couldn't leave, not after Mirabel—it would quench Seraphina. I could imagine Father sighing at my stubbornness, Mother urging me to get out.

Miss R pressed a seal upon the envelope. She walked toward me.

There may come a day when we don't have to do this. Perhaps there will be a time when we're able to act freely, when we can speak without them cutting our tongues. Until then, this is what we need to do if we are to survive.

She handed me the envelope. *Pack your bags. Do your duty.*

Clyde wrapped me in a tight embrace. A matron stood in the hall, keeping watch through the small square window.

This was your room, then? asked Clyde. *I suppose it's not horrible.*

I could have wrung his neck, but Miss R's words hovered in my mind, and I found myself swallowing my rage.

I knew you could get better, he continued. *You did it, see? There's something I want to show you.*

He took both my hands and led me to the bed, sitting us down on the unbearable springs.

You see, said Clyde, *Mister Starling wanted a cover for our latest issue. Something . . . innovative. And, well, with the moon landing and all, the other magazines were putting their girls in metallic and whatnot. Of course, being the brilliant man he is, Mister Starling didn't want to do the same, so I offered the most marvelous idea!*

Clyde reached into the pocket of his coat and unfolded a piece of paper.

Float into fashion, the cover read, *before summer ends*. And above it, a bird's-eye view of an alluring model in a scarlet swimsuit—surrounded by multicolored balloons—floating with her eyes closed in the middle of the sea.

Oh, Clyde. How desperately I wanted to choose my love, to cherish him for his attempts and let it be. I could have pretended, could have tried draining the sea in my heart and living in peace.

But alas, I could not ignore my resentment, my envy. I resented how he did not understand, envied how he would never have to.

I could hear the clinking of glass from the dining hall as the others ate their supper.

Clyde sat there looking at me, ridiculous cover in hand, and I wondered how many other visions had been twisted and robbed from their hosts.

I knew then I could not leave my sisters. All this time, the world had made me feel like I was something to be fixed. For as long as I'd lived, I was told it was *I* who needed to change. I could not let the others live the rest of their days believing there was something wrong with them too.

I asked him to leave.

He resisted, wondering why, begging me to come home.

Please, darling. I thought you'd be thrilled!

I wanted to shove him out the door, too worn to express my grievance, yet something about Miss R's ways stirred me. She had built trust through deception. How long could that prevail? Perhaps they wouldn't understand, but then we never gave them a chance to.

I explained how he had hurt me by banishing me, by treating me as a wreck and not allowing me the air I needed to surface. Our downfall was not that I had changed, but that he never tried to.

The whole damn world is a wreck! he retorted. *You can accept that or live in misery.*

He should have claimed the design as mine, should have fought for me, should have convinced others of my abilities instead of hiding me away.

You know that wouldn't work! Would you rather your ideas be executed by another or never seen at all?

He refolded the cover and slipped it into his pocket, straightening his back to compose himself as he did after every argument.

Darling, he said, lowering his voice, *you can't fight everything. You'll wear yourself out.*

He wasn't wrong. There were times I wondered how much of my strength remained, when weariness sparked a fear that I could scream as loud as the crashing waves and still, no one would listen. I dropped my gaze, stared at the scars between my toes.

Clyde lifted my chin, his coarse thumb stroking it gently.

My fear isn't that you have wild notions. It's that they'll go to waste.

He pressed his lips against my forehead, long and mournful, and I felt all our years spent together spilling away in one touch. Then he left the room, and I wept and wept, for though I was allowed to leave the pit, I did not know where to go.

When the hall was clear, I ran into the washroom. I rinsed my face, and the absurdity of washing away my tears with more salt water made me erupt into laughter. I wiped my face dry, fear sinking in. What was I to do now? I thought of giving in, of letting them carve me and rip away all that I was. Why try? What good had it gotten me?

I removed the crumpled envelope from my pocket, freedom held in my dripping hands. If I stayed, there'd be nothing I could do to prevent more women from being confined. If I left, even if I lived far away from the sea, the pit would haunt me as long as it was out there. I ran my thumb over the wax seal, felt the rippled indentations of the pearl-colored circle.

It was a wonderful marriage between Mirabel's spirit and mine, the sudden wave of inspiration that poured over me like a relentless storm. I dashed to my room and tucked the helium tank beneath my arm, sprinting back to the washroom, bathed in revelation.

I raised the tank above my head and crashed it down onto the sink's valve. Pieces of porcelain cracked and tumbled onto the floor as salt water spurt out in every direction, drenching the walls and the floor.

The rampage brought Miss R and the matrons running in, gasping as they saw the spouting scene. The water began to rise, feet soaked by my madness.

How disappointing, said Miss R. *I truly thought you'd understand.*

I kicked open a stall door.

Not another step, she warned. *I've spent half my life building this place. I won't let you destroy it!*

I entered the stall and sent the tank crashing down. Water gushed out and strengthened the deluge. She shouted at me to stop as I weaved through the rest of the stalls and showers, demanding she let the others go.

You foolish girl! cried Miss R. *That'll set us back!*

The matrons grabbed me by my arms, peeling the tank from my clawed hands.

To my office, she commanded. *Quickly!*

They dragged me down the hall. We could hear the others shouting—the flood must have flowed into the main room. The matrons held me in the office as Miss R dialed the phone upon her desk.

R, here. We've got burst pipes. I need men sent out immediately.

. . .

Lack of resources? What do you mean "lack of resources"? We'll drown!

. . .

Now, I'm sure we can come to an agreement. There are plenty of gifts I can—hello?

Wide-eyed and pale, Miss R placed the phone down on the receiver.

How could they do this? After all I've done . . .

I followed the ends of her crow's feet into her eyes, seeing fear beyond her fury. Her curled shoulders frail and drained, her voice no longer thunderous.

The matrons let go of me, trembling at the news of their doom. Screams from the main room grew louder.

I told Miss R of my plan, how it'd get us out.

No . . . no, no, no . . . she muttered, rubbing her temples. *The others . . . they're not ready.*

I hesitated before placing a hand upon her shoulder.

The more of us out there, I assured her, the more they'd have to get used to it.

She looked at me. The water embraced our knees as our fates became one.

Seraphina came running in.

What—what's happening? she quivered.

I took Seraphina's hands in mine, told her we were leaving forever.

But . . . this is my home.

I promised her she would always have a home with me, with the other women. She was meant to be out there—oh, how sorely the dreary world needed her flickering light. I told her of Helen, how she had cared for her and fought to get her out. It was time they saw each other again.

The helium tank flowed between us, knocking against our legs. I picked it up, and Seraphina's face glowed with hope.

I directed her to gather the others, to grab every sturdy object they could find and run to the second floor. Then we pushed through the water, the matrons bunching their lilac dresses around their waists.

As the others gathered what they could, I went down the hall to the other washroom, breaking more pipes. Then I trudged up the stairs, the flood chasing me up the steps. I did the same to the washrooms on the second floor, losing breath as water spurted from both floors.

Clyde could very well have been right. There was a possibility I would not exist long enough to be accepted. Yet, if that was truly the verity of our world, I didn't want to live in it.

I headed to the third-story door. The women were huddled before it, curtain rods, brooms, sewing machines in hand. The matrons gripped pots they'd once cooked our meals in. Miss R clutched a leg of her pinewood desk. She looked no different than the others, staring at me in terror alongside them.

I did not ask the women for forgiveness. I had no right to decide for them, no right to risk their souls. I feared for mine less than theirs, but I could not surrender the thought of them languishing there forever. I could not bear their visions, their beautiful eccentricities, trapped within a desolate pit so close to sea.

I swung the door open. The stairwell smelled of dust and dreams, much too dark to see its end. Water streamed down the hallway, curling itself around our ankles.

We ran. Oh, how we ran, dragging the weight with us. Up and up we climbed, hearing the crash of windows on the bottom floors breaking with every step. As the water rushed beneath us, I could see it washing over the main room in my mind, destroying the television and lifting the chairs around it. I could imagine our artwork melting into swirling ripples of color, the canvases nothing more than blotches of dripping paint. I could feel Seraphina's matches, floating alongside chess boards and books, soaked and worthless, never getting a chance to live their purpose.

We reached the top, scanning the empty attic in which Mirabel had lain many nights. She had etched her name on the wall, large and unapologetic. Vel pulled the lipstick from her pocket, scrawling below Mirabel's carvings as the letters swirled like the markings upon her skin.

Look down opon Captivity -
And laugh - No more have I

The glass pane hovered above our heads, and for a moment we stood there, gazing up at the glowing moon that suddenly seemed so close.

Stand back!

Elda, eyes fearless and determined, ripped off her feeding tubes and drove her iron stand into the window. It left a splintering mark on the glass, a spider web that glimmered against the stars. We took our gifts and knocked them against the pane, again and again, beating ourselves in the process.

One, two, black and blue.

The glass came shattering down.

I watched the women climb through the opening one by one, hoisting each other up. The water filled the attic, first to our shins, then to our stomachs. When all were out, Seraphina peeked her head through the hole and called for me. She extended her arm, waiting for me to grab it. Water hugged my chest, and Seraphina shouted, flustered over my hesitation.

The truth was, I was terrified of being wrong. As much as we despised it, the pit had kept us together. If we made it out, would there be anything to bind us? Without our doom, would we still care for each other as we did? Would we remember we were once together?

I grabbed Seraphina's hand. Miss R helped her pull me out of the crack, shards of glass slicing parts of me along the way.

As water poured out of the broken pane, I knew there was a possibility it would not flow fast enough to save us. We huddled close upon the roof, watching the salty water fill the pit we once lived in, praying there would be enough for us to swim to the edge.

The water reached our necks, and our hands slipped from the shingles. Our bodies burst outward as our cheeks swelled with air, heads bobbing up and down in colorful rhythm.

I looked to the minds around me, filled with wild ideas and oddities enough to change the world. And as I gazed at the glowing moon, its spotlight illuminating our visions, I did not know whether we would reach the top or drown. All I knew was, should I sink that night, I would have done so following the way of my soul, sputtering alongside the others, a hundred balloons let out onto the ocean.